I0831740

SNOWMAN

ALSO BY WALSH WETTENGLE

POETRY

Absinthe & Iron Cages

SNOWMAN

A Christmas Horror Story

WALSH
WETTENGLE

AEGIS
PRESS

This book is written by the author and contains no AI-generated text.

Published by:
Aegis Press, LLC
Seattle, WA
ISBN-13: 979-8-9986810-3-5
Second Edition
Cover Design by Walsh Wettengle

Dedicated to
Cleopatra and Bast,
well-missed and remembered familiars.

Love you, kitties.

Foreword

Everyone wants to write **the** novel that changes the world. Not me.

In 1990, I wanted to write a book from the perspective of a hack horror movie. We didn't call them "'80s horror movies" back then—they were just *horror movies*. Elevated Horror hadn't made its move yet, so these were all screams and fun without any psychological stakes.

I'm not sure there was ever an audience for this story—then *or* now. It has lines no one in 2025 is going to understand, like: "*He opens a phone book and flips to the yellow pages.*" For context, phone books were free hard copies of the contents of your Contacts app—if your Contacts app included every head-of-household and business in your entire city.

Ironically, I'm not even a fan of slasher films. Not much new has been done with them since the late '80s. I think *Child's Play 2* had just come out when I wrote *Snowman*, and the influence of that franchise is all over this. The slasher *wasn't human*? That was a million times better! The original films did it best, and that particular franchise (and the resulting TV series) continues to rock.

This work, perhaps, does not—but it *authentically* comes from that time. It was a blast to write it back then. Finding it again and editing it? Even better. The nostalgia hit hard—and so did the surprises. I had honestly forgotten some of the events, and completely forgotten the ending.

I didn't change any actual content, aside from a couple of names and the addition of some emotional depth to a couple of scenes that adult-me genuinely needed as a reader. Thirty-five years later I realized the Blue Moon fell on New Years Eve as 1990 took its leave and I couldn't leave that alone. Out of respect for the original manuscript, I only tweaked the flow or dialogue in a handful of places—mostly where it sounded like a 17-year-old trying to land an inside joke that didn't work. So much cringe! This was a time before we all went h-word on main (a phrase that will be long-forgotten in five years).

So, with that in mind, grab your toboggan and get ready for a bloody, horny, witchy slay ride.

-WW

Chapter 1

Scene: December 1990. The snow is falling quickly on a darkening playground. Two small boys and a small girl are finishing work on an impressive snowman.

The girl smiles as she places a second stick-arm into the snowy body.

"He's done!" gleefully boasts the girl.

"No, wait," the bigger of the two boys says. "He needs a hat!"

The smaller boy takes off his dark, rusty magenta-colored stocking cap and walks up to the snowman.

"Put my hat on Frosty, Andy," he says, shyly.

"Sure, Ricky," he says. Andy takes Ricky's hat and places it on the snowman's head.

The view changes as if someone is watching them from behind some bushes at the edge of the playground. The three children look over quickly, startled. A swing is swaying and the merry-go-round is whirling cheerily, lending a wobbling rumble to the evening air.

"It's just the wind," the girl says.

"Yeah," Ricky quickly adds.

"Well," Andy starts, "it's starting to get dark, guys." He turns to the girl. "We'd better get home, Mary."

"You're probably right," she says. "Bye Ricky, see you tomorrow."

Mary and Andy leave.

"Bye guys," Ricky whispers. He turns and stares at the snowman, standing close to say his farewell. "Bye, Frosty."

The snowman smiles.

"Bye, Ricky." Its head falls onto Ricky and crumbles.

Ricky screams. He spins away and runs to the sidewalk along the wooded area that leads away from the park. Down the sidewalk he runs in the ever-darkening, overcast twilight, struggling to catch his breath in the cold.

"I'm still with you, Ricky," comes the snowman's voice.

"No!" Ricky says and begins to cry. He slows slightly to look behind him and suddenly runs into a snowman in the middle of the sidewalk. He screams again and looks up into the charcoal briquettes they used for eyes. The snowman is wearing his hat. It bends down and picks up a hatchet. *Why was there a hatchet on the sidewalk?* Ricky barely had time to wonder to himself amidst the impossible scene.

"Merry Christmas, Ricky. Merry fucking Christmas, ha ha ha ha ha!" The snowman swings the hatchet at Ricky, knocking him to the frozen cement. Ricky gets up and runs, not realizing that his left arm, from the elbow down, is lying back on the sidewalk. He runs across someone's driveway and slips on a patch of ice. He cries out. A woman comes out of the house and sees Ricky sprawling, blood everywhere.

"Oh my God—" she screams, abruptly cut-off as a hatchet crashes into her skull. The snowman begins to slide down the driveway toward Ricky. Ricky's tears refuse to freeze on his face.

"Ricky, Ricky." The snowman chuckles. "You've been such a naughty boy! Do you know what Frosty does to naughty boys?" Ricky shakes his head. The snowman's face turns grim. "Frosty… kills them!" It raises the hatchet and brings it down with a "thunk."

Chapter 2

Scene: Morning inside a kitchen, modestly decorated for Christmas. A girl of about 17 is making breakfast. She pauses to look through the window above the sink to see it is snowing briskly—big, fluffy flakes that normally would bring a sense of peace and wonder.

"Mom!" she hollers. "Any sign of Ricky, yet?"

"No, sweetheart," her mom says shakily, entering the kitchen. "I've tried to call and see if he went to Andy's but the lines are down. If anything's happened to him—" She starts to cry.

The doorbell rings.

"I'll get it," the girl says. She goes to the door and opens it. On the stoop is a huge gift-wrapped box with a red bow on it. "Mom, I think you'd better come here!"

"What is it?" her mother asks as she comes to the door. "O-Open it." she says. The girl steps outside and pulls off the bow. She jumps back as a music-box melody to the tune of one of those old Rankin/Bass Christmas claymation specials sounds out and the box POPS open. All four sides fall to the stoop displaying the frozen, mutilated body of Ricky. They both scream. Her mom faints. They don't notice the stationary snowman in the front yard wearing Ricky's hat.

Chapter 3

Scene: The park where Ricky, Mary, and Andy built the snowman the afternoon before. Mary and Andy walk onto the playground.

"Ricky's not here, yet," Mary says, pouting. In fact, no other kids were there. Too quiet even for winter.

"Hey," Andy says, pointing to an empty space in the snow. "Our snowman is gone! Some stupid shit must've wrecked it."

"Oooooo, you said 'stupid shit'," Mary taunts him. "I'm telling Mom!"

"You are not!" Andy yells.

"Am, too," she says.

Andy packs up a snowball and nails Mary in the nose. She starts to cry and dramatically falls down. Andy pelts her with two more snowballs.

"You whore!" she yells at Andy and throws a snowball that hits him squarely in the eye.

"You stupid jerk," he yells and pounces on her.

"Get off me you child molester!" Mary gets away from him and runs, not sure if this is a game or if they are in a fight, now. The heavy, falling snow doesn't take long to begin to obscure her view. Andy runs after her and finds her climbing the ladder to the playground slide.

"I'm gonna get you!" He climbs up the ladder after her.

"Suck me," she yells. "Mom's gonna beat your ass for this!" She turns to go down the slide and sees a hat on the top of the slide. She picks it up. "Ricky's," she whispers.

Andy gets to the top.

"Got ya now!" he yells.

Mary gasps and slides down the slide. She sees a snowman at the bottom of the slide holding a hatchet. She screams as she reaches the bottom. A headless Mary crashes through the snowman as her head and the hatchet fall to the ground.

"Fuck," Andy whispers. In nauseated awe, he steps backwards where there is nowhere to step and falls from the slide. He lands on his back in a small drift. "I can't move! Help!" he cries loudly. He sees a snowman above him.

"Hello, Andy," it says. "And how are you feeling on this fine day?"

Andy screams.

"That good?" it asks. "Well, me, too. I always get this good feeling around Christmas time. Especially when it snows." It laughs. "Hmmm, Andy. You look a little numb there. Maybe you need to warm up." It stretches its stick arm unnaturally and takes a charcoal lump from where it was supposed to be an eye. The briquette glows red hot.

"We'd better get this over with soon, Andy." The snowman smiles. "Or I may just melt." It laughs. It rips open Andy's coat and sweater to place the hot coal on his chest. Andy screams hoarsely as his flesh sizzles. The snowman raises his hatchet. "Merry Christmas," it says and crashes the hatchet down.

Ricky's sister enters the park and hears Andy's final scream. The snow continues to fall heavily.

"Hello?" she asks. "Who's here?" She runs toward the scream and trips over Mary's head. She dusts the snow from her coat and gets back up without noticing what she tripped over. Her eyes are riveted to what appears to be a kid lying in the snow. She approaches Andy's body which is now face down in the snow and wearing Ricky's hat.

"Andy?" she asks. "Is that you?" She reaches down to nudge him and takes a deep breath before turning him over. Two coals exist where his eyes were. The girl screams. She turns to run and crashes into the snowman. It whips her across the face with its stick arms, drawing blood. She screams again and runs.

"Come back soon!" the snowman screams.

Ricky's sister reaches her house, runs in, and slams the door. Her father enters the entry hall where she stands, unable to bring herself to move.

"You'd better get moving if you want to be ready for the service, Amy," he says.

"But," she pleads. Her fathers leaves. She slowly moves into their living room and is able to bring herself to look out the bay window. The snowman is there, inches from the glass.

"Merry Christmas, Amy," it says. "Won't you come out and play?"

Amy screams and her mom comes running into the room.

"What is it?" her mom asks. "Amy?"

"A snowman!" Amy screams. Her mom looks out the window and sees a typical, shoddily-crafted snowman in the middle of the yard.

"Yes, that's what it is, Amy," her mom says, emptiness in her voice. "What's wrong? Are you sure you want to go to the service? This is impossibly hard on all of us and I would understand if it's too much. I don't know how I am going to make it through."

"Yes, I'm OK," Amy answers. After filling a small bag with some of Ricky's mementos, Amy and her parents get into their car and leave.

Chapter 4

Scene: It's dusk. Two teens are walking down Amy's street with that look about them that parents seem to think spells *trouble* in white kids, and it usually does. One 18 year-old with long, brown hair in Wranglers and a jean jacket with fake white fur along the collar. The other, a 17 year-old with short, black hair, wore Lee jeans and a worn-out leather motorcycle jacket. Neither could be very warm in this weather but sometimes one's look is more important. Another 16 year-old teen runs to catch up with them, Black with short-cropped hair, and wearing baggy jeans with a red, flannel jacket.

"Wait up!" he yells.

"Well, hurry the fuck up, Jerry!" the short-haired kid yells back.

"Hey, Cory, look." The long haired kid points.

Cory gasps. "Fuckin-A, Dave. It's a snowman!" Jerry catches up with them both.

"Let's trash it!" Jerry claps his hands.

"Hell yeah," Dave says, mockingly. "Let's kill the snowman." He runs up to it and gives a high kick to the head. Its head crumbles as Jerry and Cory then forcefully sandwich it and fall into the heap of snow. Cory gets up.

"Hey, where'd *that* snowman come from?" He points behind Dave. Dave turns around and faces another snowman.

"Woah. As God is my shitness," Dave says, "it was not here a second ago!"

"Well, let's bust it." Jerry moves forward.

"How'bout, I bust you?" the snowman asks.

"What the fuck?" Cory exclaims.

Jerry gulps. "That shit ain't on!"

"Merry Christmas, boys." The snowman picks up a hatchet. Jerry screams and runs off.

"C'mon, Dave," Cory yells. "Let's mosh!"

"Holy fuck," Dave whispers in fear.

"Not a holy one," the snowman says. "A cold one!" It swings the hatchet into Dave's left arm. Dave falls and screams.

"Dave!" Cory screams. "Get up!" Dave gets to his feet as the snowman begins to swing its hatchet again. Cory jumps at the snowman and tears out one of its stick arms. In return, the snowman swings his hatchet into Cory's gut. Cory collapses as Dave runs off, trying not to trip over himself in the snow.

Meanwhile, Jerry is walking rapidly down the street. "I knew I shouldn't have gone with those dudes!" Suddenly, he hears Dave call his name.

"Jerry!"

"Oh, shit," Jerry mutters. He runs toward where he last saw Dave and Cory. He finds himself in the yard where the snowman was and sees a hand sticking out of a snowdrift. "Oh hell, who is that? Cory?"

He pulls the hand out and realizes it is disembodied. He yelps as he drops it. "Oh shit! Mother of fuck!"

"Hello, Jerry. Nice night, isn't it?" came a voice. Jerry whirls around to face… nothing? "Up here, Jerry," came the voice again.

Jerry looks up. In a tree he sees a blood-stained snowman holding something round and furry, like a maniacal cherry Slush Puppy. Jerry turns to run.

"Oh, Jerry," the snowman cries. "Wait! Cory wanted to say

something to you." Jerry turns back to the tree as the snowman hurls its round object at him. With utter horror, Jerry sees that it's Cory's head.

"JERRY!!!!" the head screams. It hits Jerry in the chest and falls to the ground. Jerry runs again. He's never run this fast before.

"Oh God, oh fuck oh damn, oh Hell, oh, oh!!" Jerry cries as he runs.

"Jerry..." a voice cries. Jerry looks behind him and with a sick fascination he sees Cory's head rolling along behind him. "Help me, Jerry. The snowman killed me. Now, he's going to kill you! Ha Ha Ha! Merry Christmas, Jerry! Merry—"

"Shut up!" Jerry cries. "Just shut the fuck up!" He stops, spins around, and delivers the kick-of-his-life to Cory's head. The head flies through the air and the snowman catches it.

"That wasn't nice to kick your friend so close to Christmas, Jerry," it taunts. "Maybe I'll come down your chimney instead of Santa."

"I'll be sure to light the fire, fucker!" Jerry cries.

"Oh no." The snowman looks surprised. "That won't do at all. I could melt." He produces his hatchet.

"No, no, motherfucker..." Jerry, cries hysterically. "You just get that hatchet the fuck away from me!"

"Jerry, Jerry," the snowman shakes his head. "Where's your Christmas Spirit?" He slides toward Jerry.

"Get the hell back," Jerry blubbers.

The snowman starts to sing. "Deck the halls with Jerry's innards. Fa la la la la la la la la. He makes quite a good Christmas dinner. Fa la la la la la la la."

"No!" Jerry cries. The snowman strikes Jerry in the shoulder with the hatchet. Jerry screams, blood gurgling in his mouth.

The snowman keeps singing.

"But now he's writhing on the ground in pain. Fa la la la la la la la la." The snowman keeps hacking away and singing. "Because the snowman likes to kill and maim. Fa la la la la la la la la!" He laughs maniacally.

Chapter 5

Scene: Amy and her parents pull into their driveway following Ricky's services. Her mother's eyes are red and distant from crying. Amy's parents enter the house as Amy walks into the front yard.

"Oh, Ricky," she whispers like a sigh. She walks over to where Cory, Dave, and Jerry trashed the yard snowman. She kneels down at the sight of the frozen blood in the snow. She touches it and gasps.

"It killed someone else," she whispers. As she begins to walk into the house she sees Cory's hand on the front walk. She gags and runs to the side of the house where she nearly pukes. She walks around to the back of her house, trying to keep her stomach contents down. She stifles a scream as she sees a body sprawled in the snow in her backyard. She runs over to where he lies, his jean jacket covered in his blood. She touches the wound on his shoulder and he cries out.

"You're alive?" she asks. He grabs her.

"A snowman. Run," he pleads.

"I know," she stammers. "It killed my brother. I'm Amy."

"I'm… I'm Dave." He lies back down.

"And you need a doctor," she adds.

Chapter 6

Scene: The next day. Amy's house.

Dave walks up to Amy's front door and rings the doorbell. Amy answers.

"Dave?" she asks, to be sure. "Come in."

They go into the kitchen and sit.

"Where's your folks?" he asks.

"They just found my brother's friends' bodies at the park and my mom and dad went to support their parents and demand some answers from the police."

"Well," Dave says,"I know Cory's dead. I think Jerry is, too, because on the news it said pieces of a kid were found six blocks from here."

"That is sick," she says.

"What is this thing?" Dave asks.

"I don't know," Amy says, "but it kills kids and it killed my brother. Someone has to stop it."

Chapter 7

Scene: A small girl is in her backyard. She's holding a doll and making a small snowman almost her own size. It's snowing.

"Maryanne," she says to the doll. "Frosty wants to have tea. Wait here with him." She sits the doll next to the child-size snowman and goes inside. She enters a kitchen. "Mommy! I need some tea for Maryanne and Frosty!"

"Okay, Carrie," her mom says. Her mom pours cold water from the tap into a pitcher. "Here you go, Carrie."

"That's not tea, Mommy," Carrie says. "It's just water."

"Yes," Mommy says, "but it's magic water. If you pour the water over Frosty, he'll turn into magic ice, okay?"

"Oh," Carrie says. "Okay!" Carrie takes the pitcher and goes outside. When she goes into the backyard, she sees the snowman is holding her doll.

"Frosty!" she scolds. "Why'd you take Maryanne?" She takes Maryanne out of its arms and places her at the base of a tree. She pours the pitcher over the snowman. As she does this, she notices a hat half-buried in the snow. She walks over and picks it up. She has no way of knowing that it is Ricky's hat.

"Perfect!" she exclaims. She puts it on the snowman's head.

The wind picks up, blowing snow from the surface of the drifts in the backyard. Carrie goes to pick up Maryanne and drops the pitcher when she sees Maryanne has grown to her size.

"I want my tea, Carrie," Maryanne says. "You promised me tea. If you don't keep to your promise, Santa won't bring you any toys. And you promised Frosty, too." Carrie tums to look at her small snowman, but it remains unanimated.

"Didn't she promise you, Frosty?" Maryanne walks up to the snowman and puts her arms around it. She kisses it deep and starts to caress it. The snowman's stick-arms wrap around Maryanne. She begins to buck against it screaming, "Oh! Oh! Ha ha ha!"

Maryanne and the snowman stop abruptly and both turn to look directly at Carrie. Carrie immediately runs toward the house.

Maryanne and the snowman run after her.

"Come back, Carrie!" the snowman screams. "It's your turn!" Carrie reaches the door just as Maryanne reaches Carrie. Maryanne throws Carrie down.

"You bitch," Maryanne says. "First, you promised me tea and now you try to steal my man. You. Slut."

Carrie starts to cry and stands back up.

"I'll fight you for him, Carrie." Maryanne holds up her fabric fists. "Whoever wins can fuck out his brains." Maryanne punches Carrie who falls back down.

"Maryanne, that wasn't nice!" the snowman cries. "I hope Santa Clause sees how you've been acting."

"Frosty?" Maryanne asks as it picks up an ax.

"It's time to go back to the cabbage patch, Maryanne," the snowman says as it axes Maryanne's stuffing-filled head clean off, sending blood flying everywhere. Carrie screams.

"What's wrong, Carrie?" the snowman asks as Carrie runs again toward the house. "Carrie! Come Back!" The snowman cackles after her, singing "Over the river and through the woods to Grandmother's house we go!" It is suddenly in front of her.

"Merry Christmas, Carrie." It swings the ax.

Chapter 8

Scene: Carrie's mother steps into her backyard from the door off the kitchen.

"Carrie?" she calls. "Carrie, where are you?"

She looks at her feet and sees the beheaded Maryanne doll which has returned to its normal size. The ground around it is covered in the expected snow, with no blood in sight.

"Carrie?" she whispers and runs back inside. Through a window we see her dialing a phone number on her marigold-colored kitchen phone. The view of the window enlarges as whoever's eyes we are looking through rushes toward it. Then from the inside, Carrie's mother turns toward the window, stretching the coiled cord between the wall and the handset. She looks out and drops the phone which rebounds back to the wall with a thud. She emits a piercing scream as an ax crashes through the window and the snowman follows it through with a flurry of snow. Its smaller form has blood splotched across its iced surface. The blood and outer surface of the ice begin to drip as it lowers itself to the kitchen floor. Carrie's mother runs down a hall. The snowman slowly leaves a trail of melting slush as it follows.

Dashing into a bathroom, she attempts to slam the door closed as an ax splinters the bottom hinge from the door. She screams again. She reaches into the shower and turns on the water. Grabbing the handheld shower head attachment from its cradle, she pulls it from the shower and aims it at the snowman. It raises its ax only to drop it to the floor as she douses the snowman in a spray of hot water. Silently, it melts, leaving behind an ax, two sticks, two small rock eyes, and a baby carrot. She quickly scoops up the leftover features and dumps them out the kitchen door. She sighs, not quite in relief but to just breathe normally again, and closes the door. She is back in the safety of the house and the shards of glass spread across the kitchen floor.

Outside, the snow where the items were dumped begins to shape and grow until it becomes the form of the snowman. It's holding the ax.

Carrie's mother is dialing on the phone, again. The snowman drags its ax across the siding next to the back door and severs the cable where the telephone line enters the house.

"Hello?" asks the mother into the phone. "Hello?"

Her face turns grave. She goes to the back door, looks through the glass storm door, and starts. She sees the bare spot in the snow where she dumped the pieces of the snowman. She locks the door and runs to the front room of the house. She looks out several windows before opening the front door. She opens it and looks into the driveway. Stepping onto the front step, she takes one last look and then runs for her car. When she reaches it, she tries to open the door. It is frozen shut. She emits a cry.

"Oh, fuck, open," she sobs. She keeps trying the door. A snowball suddenly hits her on the shoulder. She screams.

"Who's there?" she asks. Another snowball whizzes past her and hits the car. "Stop it!" she wails. The bushes behind her shake, scattering snow to the ground. A snowball hits her in the face. Then two small boys run out from behind the bushes, laughing. They run down the street..

"You little brats!" Carrie's mother hollers after them. She gives one last yank on the car door. It opens. "Thank God," she mutters. A snowball hits the back of her head. "You little shits!" she screams as she spins around to face the snowman.

She screams again as it brings its ax down.

It shatters her car window.

She runs.

"Aren't you going to go caroling with me?" the snowman asks. It pursues her. Carrie's mother is running down the street until she slips on a patch of ice. She gets up and runs for about a block, then she slips again. She screams for help.

Across the street, through a kitchen window, Dave and Amy look up from a conversation. They are sitting across a table from each other.

"Did you hear something?" Amy asks. Through the window, Carrie's mother is standing back up on the sidewalk.

"I'm not sure," Dave replies.

The snowman is sliding toward Carries's mother with its ax raised.

"Maybe I'm just jumpy, considering everything," says Amy.

Carrie's mother runs across the street and through the yard towards the kitchen window. She has blood all over her.

"Yeah, I guess that makes sense," Dave says.

Carrie's mother thumps against the window. Dave and Amy look over, startled. They both scream. The snowman raises its ax over Carrie's mother's head. The THUNK could be heard inside the house as Carrie's mother collapses into the snow. The snowman crashes his ax through the kitchen window.

"Dave! Amy!" he cackles. "I see you've met. Well, come here I got a gift for you. It's from Ricky, Amy!"

Dave and Amy start to flee but Amy turns to face the snowman. She begins to shake as if in a full-body spasm.

"Come on out, Amy!" the snowman taunts.

"Amy!" Dave hollers. He grabs her arm and leads her out of the kitchen. He takes her into a bedroom and lies her down on a bed. "Amy, wake up!"

She blinks.

"Dave?" she begins to cry. He puts his arms around her.

"How sweet!" The snowman comes into the room. Amy sees

Ricky's hat on him and yells in rage.

"What are you?" Dave asks.

"Why," the snowman cocks its head, "I'm a snowman, silly."

Amy stands up. "How many have you killed?" she screams.

"Oh, since Ricky, Andy, and Mary built me? About eight. I'm ready to go for a ten, though." It brandishes its ax.

Dave attempts to tackle the snowman and grab the ax. They're both holding onto it.

"Dave!" Amy screams. She reaches for the snowman's hat. "That's Ricky's hat!" She almost reaches it.

"NO!" the snowman bellows. "Don't touch that hat, you bitch!" It lets go of the ax and grabs Amy.

Dave seizes the ax from the floor and severs the stick-arm that had fastened onto Amy. The snowman turns toward Dave. It makes a snowball from its body with its remaining stick-arm and hurls it at Dave's face.

"Shit," Dave mutters. The snowman rushes at him as Dave plunges the ax right through its body. A light spray of blood lands on Dave's face. The snowman wraps its stick-hand around Dave's neck. Amy eyes a Windsor chair next to the bed. She quickly picks it up and raises it above the snowman's head.

"Die!" she murderously screams. She brings the chair down with all of her strength and crashes it through the snowman's head, crumbling it. It carries through to hit Dave in the head knocking him unconscious. The entire snowman crumbles.

"Dave," she says as she kneels next to him. "Wake up." She takes some snow and rubs it on Dave's face and forehead, hoping the cold will wake him up. Instead, the snow becomes blood and Amy draws back, frightened. The mass of snow, including the ax, the hat, carrot, coals, and stick, began to crawl toward the bedroom door. Amy jumps on the mass and begins to stomp, frantically. The lone stick-arm reaches for the ax and the snowman's face assembles itself together on top of the snow pile.

"Hi Amy," the face giggles. Amy lets out a hastily gasped scream. The snow pile trips her with the ax and she hits her head in the door frame. She collapses to the floor as the snowman's crumbled form flows from the house.

Chapter 9

Amy's eyes flutter open. She gets up, looks at Dave, who is starting to wake up, and runs after the snowman. She gets outside just as the sliding snow pile hits the snow in the front yard. It begins to grow into the familiar form of a snowman. Amy grabs the hat as the snowman grabs her arm.

"I told you this is *my* hat," it growls. "Kids today never listen!"

Dave runs out of the house toward the fray.

"Dave, help!" Amy shouts. Dave grabs the snowman's single stick-arm and pulls it out of its body. A small amount of blood pumps out, then freezes. Amy takefs the hat from the snowman.

"Nooo—" the snowman becomes completely stiff. Its face becomes lifeless.

"Yes!" Amy cries. "We did it!" She begins to bawl. Dave embraces her.

"It was the hat?" Dave asks.

"Yes," Amy says between sobs. "Just—like in—the song. It was Ricky's hat."

"But, why?" Dave asks. "How come Ricky's hat is so special?" Dave takes Ricky's hat from Amy. "How long had Ricky had this hat?"

"Mom bought it the morning of the day he died," she says. She was beginning to compose herself, her sobs were fewer now. "From the second hand store on 30th street." Dave takes Amy inside. They walk past Carrie's mother and her blood frozen into the snow. He looks at the blood, then at the hat. The colors are the same. He runs inside to the kitchen and tums on the water faucet. He saturates the hat then puts it to his nose and lips.

"Dave?" questions Amy.

"It's blood," Dave gasps. He scrubs the hat with some dish soap. It leaves a slightly faded spot on the hat. "It's dyed with blood!" He drops it. Blood is on his hands. Blood then begins to pour from the water faucet. Amy gasps. It begins to snow quite heavily outside. Amy and Dave start to shiver as snow blows in from the broken kitchen window. The sink fills with blood and it begins to freeze.

"Dave!" Amy points at the sink. Dave tries to take the hat but it's partially frozen in the bloody ice. A frozen blood hand reaches from the sink and grabs his wrist. He shrieks. A humanoid head, also of frozen blood, rises from the sink.

"You can never win, fools," it says. "You cannot defeat me!" A full-size man consisting of blood-ice climbs out of the sink into the kitchen. He is semi-transparent and taller than both of the teens.

The hat can be seen embedded in his chest where a person's heart would be. It pulses grotesquely, rhythmically.

"Run!" Dave yells and takes off. Amy turns to run and smacks into the frame of the kitchen entryway. She grunts.

"Amy," pants the iceman. "How about somethin' a little cold in your pants?" It grasps its crotch and a bloody ice-phallus forms.

Amy's eyes bulge and she screams.

Chapter 10

Dave is outside searching insanely through the snow. Finally, he finds what he is looking for. The ax.

Chapter 11

Amy tries to run from the iceman but it grabs her arm. She can feel its ice-prick against her glutes.

She screams again and Dave runs back in with the ax.

"Go away," the iceman says. "We're busy."

The iceman's form is more definite now. Its muscles and fleshly features are well-defined in this blood-filled, frozen form.

Dave thunders the ax toward the iceman, but the living blasphemy easily disarms Dave and propels him into the kitchen table. Dave's wound on his arm opens and starts to bleed, the pain racking his brain.

The iceman picks up the ax. Dave ducks under the table as the ax splits it in half.

"NO!" Amy screams. "Stop it!" She grabs a butcher's knife from a countertop knife block and tries to hack at the iceman. Instead, she only chips a piece from its back. It gasps in outrage, not pain, as blood trickles from the wound.

"Damn!" it cries in an other-worldly voice. It backhands her and she falls to the floor, dropping the knife, apparently unconscious. Dave picks up a kitchen chair and tries to ward off the ice-thing. The iceman crashes its foot through the chair, sending splinters everywhere.

Chapter 12

A car pulls into the driveway and Amy's mother and father get out. They hear a crash and notice the kitchen window is broken. Then, they notice the body of Carrie's mother. Amy's mother screams as her father runs inside.

Amy's father runs into the kitchen and his jaw drops, his mouth agape in shock. The iceman turns toward him and buries the ax into his chest. He gags and collapses. Dave shoves the iceman with whatever little strength he has left. The iceman trips over Amy's gurgling, dying father and sprawls onto the ground.

The struggle carries into the front room of the house as Amy's mother is entering from outside. She wails at the sight of the iceman. The iceman stands and lunges at her.

"Fucking banshee," it mutters. It pushes her into the yard. "I'll kill you."

It begins to rip at her clothes. Dave goes to Amy.

"Amy. Amy, wake up," he cries. She opens her eyes. "Come on." They go out the back door.

The iceman is still pounding on Amy's mother with its frozen fists. "Merry Christmas, bitch!" it expresses and then looks toward the house. Its features are becoming slightly undefined and its reddish color is starting to vanish from its translucent form. It goes into Amy's kitchen and picks up her butcher knife. It makes a laceration with the knife on its left ankle. Blood gushes from the chipped ice and its color quickly pales. It stands like this until it is as crystal clear as fresh ice and its core turns a splintered frozen white. The hat can now only barely be seen in its chest.

Chapter 13

Dave and Amy are running, trying to put distance between them and the house.

"Any physical form it takes must be made of ice or snow," Amy pants, trying to piece it all together.

"Sorta figured that out," Dave replies. "So we wait until Spring? Great! It's December now."

"No, we can't run forever," she says and slows down to a walk. "We have to kill it."

"How?" Dave asks. "The hat is buried in its chest!"

"We have to melt it," Amy says.

"Oh great." Dave looks to the sky. "Let's go to Shopko and buy a flame-thrower! Or better yet, when the New Age people and the witches get together to walk over burning coals next week, we'll invite the snowman along! Brilliant, Amy!"

"Dammit, Dave!" Amy screams. "Why are you such an asshole!?" She starts to cry.

"I'm sorry, Amy," he says. "It's just that I'm freaking out. Things like this aren't supposed to happen!"

"We need help," Amy says. Then her eyes light up.

"Did you say, New Age people and witches?"

Chapter 14

Dave and Amy are climbing in a bedroom window. Dave starts to undress. Amy blushes and turns away. She looks around the room and notices several posters, Megadeth, Ozzy, Anthrax, Iron Maiden, Lizzy Borden, and Black Sabbath. She also notices a stunning view of Dave's butt as he changes out of his bloody, wet clothes.

"Here," he says as he hands her a shirt and pants. "These should fit you."

"Thanks." She hesitates before undressing, then shrugs before quickly changing clothes. Dave takes her clothes and puts them under his bedsheets.

"In case my mom or dad decides to search my room," he says.

He opens a phone book and flips to the Yellow Pages.

"Now, where do we even get ahold of a witch?" Amy asks.

"I'm not too sure," he says. "But, there is an occult bookstore on Farnum Street." He flips a couple pages. "Here we are: Covenstead Metaphysical Supply Center."

"I hope this is worth it," she starts to climb out the window. Dave puts his arms around her waist. She turns around and they both subject themselves to a 20-second mission of exploring the inside of each other's mouths.

"Wait outside," Dave says. "I've got to find out if I can borrow the car."

Amy climbs out the window.

Chapter 15

Dave pulls the car into a street parking stall in front of a historic brick building with a sign saying "Covenstead Books & Supplies". The clock at the bank across the street says 5:30 PM.

"Tomorrow's Christmas Eve," Amy observes as she exits the vehicle.

"Good," Dave says. "My parents will be in church all day, bible bangin'."

"I take it you're not religious?" Amy asks.

"Not if I can help it," he says. "Christianity is too backwards for me." They walk into Covenstead. The scents of incense and dried herbs immediately fill their senses.

The shop is quite spacious. Bookcases line the back of two walls. Occult, pagan, and Native American artifacts and decor line the front of the store. It is dimly lit and when their eyes adjust to the light, they notice that only candles and small, dimmed lamps light the room. Through another doorway, a small herbal dispensing and grow light area can be seen. The special this week, written on a small chalkboard, is *Live European Mandrake Root*. Another doorway is blocked by a curtain.

Dave and Amy both feel lighter and safer after walking into the store and giving it a once-over. A woman of about 40, comes into the room from behind the curtain. She is wearing a purple and white robe decorated with symbols of Wiccan, Celtic, Druidic, and Egyptian influence. An eclectic melting pot of symbolism, to be sure.

"Greetings," she says and smiles. "My name is Rowena. How may I be of service?"

"Are you a witch?" Amy quickly asks.

"Why, yes," she exclaims. "I am a student of Wicca, Witchcraft, and other Neo-Pagan religions."

"We need help," Dave says. "We're being pursued by a paranormal being, or a demon, or... something!"

"It's killed at least eight people!" Amy cries.

"Okay, calm down," Rowena hastily says. "Come with me." She parts the curtain and ushers them through.

The room behind the curtain was even more enchanting than the rest of the storefront.

A stained-glass window covered most of the back wall. The design included a pentagram with a series of abstract designs and colors surrounding it. Along one wall was a desk and bookshelf filled with books from psychometry and divination to weather manipulation. Along another wall was a huge painting of a witches' Sabbat and a stairway to a second floor. Along the last wall was a couch, a table, and a refrigerator. In the middle of the room was a giant rug with concentric Celtic circles in its design, a long table, and a man sitting in a comfy armchair.

The man looked like he had to be quite old, except his face and body were young. His beard was white as ivory and went midway down his chest. His white hair was 2-3 inches past his shoulders. He was dressed in a black and white flowing robe and looked stunningly elegant and wise. A pentagram necklace hung around his neck.

"Ránulf," Rowena addressed the man. "We have guests. Names please?" she asks them.

"Uh, Amy and Dave," Dave says. Instantly, the "old" man perks up.

"Ránulf?" Dave says, recalling a TV interview from earlier in the year. "I've heard of you. You made the 10:00 news for defending the library's decision not to ban anything from its book collection when the church was protesting them. I thought you looked like someone from a Dio video!"

"Heard o' old Ránulf Wylkyn, have ye?" Ránulf asks. "Reckon I'm not forgotten yet. What sort o' mess brings ye to me door, then?"

"Wait, wait," Rowena interrupts. "Sit, children. Make ye—I mean, *yourselves* at home."

"Aye, aye," Ránulf mutters 'twixt puffs of his corncob pipe. "Hurry up, then. Tha knows I've nowt but time 'til Samhain to hear your story."

Chapter 16

Dave and Amy slowly unfold their tale of terror as Rowena and Ránulf occasionally give each other knowing, fearful glances. Amy is in tears at the end of the story. Rowena rests her hand on Amy's forearm to comfort her.

"Well, do you believe us?" Dave asks.

"Of course we do, David!" Rowena assures him. Ránulf gives her a dirty look and goes back to playing with a pendulum on a nearby table. "Don't we, Rán?" she asks.

"Ye say the hat giveth life to the snowman?" Ránulf asks.

"Yes," Dave but David-for-the-moment answers.

"It was dyed with blood?" Ránulf asks.

"Yes," David answers.

"Ye're certain it was a snowman?" Ránulf asks.

"Yes!" David almost screams.

"Steady on, lad," Ránulf says. "No need to shout."

"So, can you help us, Ránulf?" Amy asks.

"I'll need time," he says, sighing. "But I'm sure I can help ye. For now, take these." He hands each of them a necklace with a silver, interwoven pentacle on it. "Wear these. They should permit the snowman to forget ye for a time."

"But for now I insist you stay with us," Rowena interjects, rising from her seat.

"But… my parents," Amy cries. "They're dead and what about the police?"

Ránulf gives Rowena another nasty look. "Ye can take this one, Rowena. I have studying to do." He ascends the staircase, out-of-sight. Rowena opens a hidden cabinet and lifts out a black & white marble crystal of some sort.

"Amy," she says. "Your parents died in a fire." The crystal glows from the inside. Rowena puts her hands around it. "You're staying with friends to recover from your grief." She looks at Dave. "Call your parents and tell them you're staying at a friend's." She points to the curtain. "The phone is by the front counter in the shop." She puts the crystal back.

"Did you make my house burn?" Amy asks.

Rowena nods. "Otherwise the police would make the situation worse," she says.

Dave locates the phone and dials his home. While he waits for one of his folks to pick up, he sees a stack of fliers for a talk being put on by the bookstore: *The Old Ways in the New World: A Conversation with Ránulf Wylkyn*.

When Dave comes back from the phone, Rowena locks up the store and takes them upstairs to a guest room. "I hope you don't mind sleeping together," Rowena whispers. "We only have this one extra bed." Ránulf comes in.

"Nay, lad!" he barks. "David, tha'll be takin' t'sofa tonight." Ránulf goes into a neighboring room. It's set up like a library study. Books and newspaper racks line the walls. Ránulf takes some newspapers from a file. His face turns grave as he looks at them. Rowena enters. He picks up a staff from where it was resting against the wall and extinguishes his pipe.

"Where are you going?" Rowena asks.

"If this incarnation is what I think it is," he says, "then I must see it for myself. Watch the kids, will ye?" He leaves.

Rowena walks over to the papers Ránulf was reading. The headline reads: "COPS SLAY SATANIC SORCERER." Another one reads: "INFANT SLAIN BY DEMONIC INVOKER." The color drains from her face.

Chapter 17

Two elementary-aged boys and a girl are behind a stout snow wall. Snowballs occasionally fly above them.

"They're beating us, Tim!" one boy cries.

"Shut up, Brian! We can still wi—" a snowball hits him in the mouth. He backs over and lands on his butt. They put their backs to the snow fort.

"Should we run?" the girl asks.

"Wait, Jamie," Brian says. "They've stopped."

"Everybody grab some snow!" Tim calls out as he runs

toward the other snow fort. Brian and Jamie each grab snow and follow Tim.

"Cowabunga!" Brian screams. Tim gets to the other fort first and screams as he sees the dead bodies of three other kids. Brian stops short but Jamie runs up to Tim. She shrieks.

Suddenly, out of the snow, the iceman grabs Tim. All three children shriek in unison, sounding off like a bizarre, horror choir. Tim screams again and defecates. Brian runs away.

"Stop it!" Jamie cries. "Stop! Stop! Stop!" and "Help!"

"Shut up, you little slore," the ice-being growls. "I'm going to kill you, too." It reaches for her coat and catches its hand on her hood as she starts to run. She chokes—then screams. Tim is crying.

Chapter 18

Brian is running down the street and slams into an old, bearded man, Ránulf.

"Woah," Ránulf says soothingly. "What's the matter, lad?"

"A-a monster! Help!" the lad pleads. "It's got m-my friends!"

"Ye stay here," Ránulf says.

Chapter 19

The iceman is holding onto Jamie with one hand and Tim with the other. It pushes Tim's head into the snow, burying it.

"Smother, you little brat!" the iceman cries. "Die, so I can feed on your life's essence!"

A snowball hits the ice incarnation in the face. It drops both kids. Tim has fainted. Jamie squats and cries, not aware that she has wetted.

"Who?" the iceman howls. "Someone dares?"

"Aye." Ránulf appears from behind the other fort. "Just me."

"Beat it, old man," the iceman says. "I don't go for senior citizens."

Ránulf sticks his staff in the snow and begins to work his fingers and mutter under his breath. His eyes blaze and his fingers glow as he points at the ice blasphemy. A beam of electric blue light emits itself from Ránulf's index finger and hits the iceman in the chest. The iceman shrieks as it glows blue for an instant. It drops to one knee.

"Hmmm," mutters Ránulf. The iceman points its left hand at Ránulf and three ice daggers shoot toward him. The first one embeds itself in Ránulf's left shoulder. The second one misses, and the third one falls into the snow as Ránulf raises his hand with a dismissive gesture toward it.

"Gods," Ránulf mutters. He wraps both hands around his staff.

"You should have fled when I gave you a chance, wizard!" the ice thing warns.

"Ye should return to whatever infernal realm ye originated from," Ránulf replies back, spit flying with his words.

The ice thing rushes at Ránulf and he deflects it expertly with his staff. Then, Ránulf staffs the ice thing in its chest, shattering ice and exposing part of the hat. The iceman howls. Ránulf tries to strike it again, but crumples because of the wound in his shoulder. The iceman wastes no time and attacks. Ránulf's eyes widen as he tries to duck the assault. Instead of hitting him in the jaw, the iceman bludgeons Ránulf's chest. The breath leaves Ránulf as he flies into the snow fort.

"I don't get much pleasure in killing old men," the ice thing snarls. "Children have much more life to take away!"

"I've plenty enough life in me, yet," Ránulf growls between gasps. "More than enough to banish the likes o' ye!" He reaches into his robe and produces a small obsidian sphere. The iceman lunges at the wizard and Ránulf semi-impales the ice demon with his staff and flips him over his back. The iceman lands on its chest and quickly turns over.

"Damn you to Hell!" it screams.

"Hell is only a state of mind," Ránulf says, wisely. He tosses the obsidian orb at the iceman where it embeds in his chest. The iceman instantly petrifies where it lies. Jamie stands up.

"Is it dead?" she asks with a sob.

"Nay," Ránulf answers. "That thing'll just hold the soul for a bit. Now, let's see to thy friend." Ránulf walks over to Tim.

"You're hurt." Jamie notices his shoulder wound. He takes a small jar and a bandage from another pocket inside his robe. He rubs
some salve from the jar onto the bandage, then sticks it under his robe onto his injured shoulder.

"What is that?" Jamie nods, indicating the salve.

"It is a healing compound," Ránulf answers. "Made only with the finest of herbs." He kneels beside Tim.

"E's in fine fettle," he grunts as Tim stirs. "Just needed wakin'. Hurry along home, now, the both of ye." The children run off.

"It's black o'er Bill's mother's," Ránulf mutters, squinting at the darkening clouds over the horizon. "We've not seen the last of this storm, nor the likes o' *him*."

Chapter 20

It's about 8:00 PM as Ránulf returns to the store. Dave starts as Ránulf parts the curtain and comes into the room.

"You scared me," Dave says. "I thought you were the snowman." He sits up on the couch. A fire in a wood burning stove is giving the room an eerie glow.

"Nay," Ránulf says, voice low and steady. "It is only me. Ye are safe from the 'snowman' as long as ye are guests in my home. Evil entities are not permitted here."

Dave looks at Ránulf's shoulder. "What happened?" he asks, worried.

"Just a scratch," Ránulf reassures him. "Nothing auric healing can't take care of. Good night, David." Ránulf ascends the stairs.

"Good night," Dave replies.

Chapter 21

Later in the night, Dave awakens. He remembers Amy saying "we have to melt it." He lights a candle and goes to the bookshelf.

"*Herb Magic*," he reads. "*Astral Projection, Complete Book of Witchcraft, Complete Works of Crowley, Tarot Spells*. Ah! *Weather Manipulation*!" He takes the small hardbound book from the shelf and sits in Ránulf's chair. He sits there in his underwear and begins to read to himself. He turns the pages, *Summoning*

Rain, Halting Rain, Summoning Winds, Calming Winds, then he stops on the page reading *Dispelling Cold.*

Then suddenly Ránulf is before him, smoking his corn cob pipe. Dave gasps in shock. "I-I didn't hear you come down," he says.

"I studied with cats back in the green and pleasant land," Ránulf says, puffing lightly. He looks at the book and then at Dave. "Think on, soft lad. Ye cannot change the seasons, son. The Goddess' mind can't be changed against Her will."

"Goddess?" Dave asks.

"Aye," Ránulf answers. "The Earthmother, commonly known to Christians and atheists as Mother Nature."

"Oh," Dave says, not yet completely understanding.

"Now I suggest ye get some sleep," Ránulf advises. "Come morning, I shall inform ye of what ye and thy girlfriend are up against."

Dave lies back on the couch as Ránulf turns to go. Ránulf steals a look back and notices *Weather Manipulation* open to *Dispelling Cold.* He picks it up and goes back upstairs.

Chapter 22

It is the morning of Christmas Eve. Rowena descends the stairs and walks over to Dave. She places her hand on his shoulder.

"Dave," she whispers. "David, wake up!" She shakes him and he turns over and grumbles. "Morning feast is ready upstairs... and Ránulf wishes to speak with you." He gets up as she lights some incense and goes into the store. He dresses and goes upstairs.

Ránulf and Amy are already in the library study. Ránulf is shuffling a deck of Tarot cards. He hands them to Amy with a book entitled *The Witches Sacred Tarot* depicting someone looking a bit like Ránulf holding a ritual dagger above a chalice.

"Good morning," Ránulf cheerily greets him. "There's blueberry muffins made from scratch." He gestures toward them.

"Thanks." Dave engages in eating.

"Here," Ránulf hands Dave a copy of *Complete Book of Witchcraft*. "Ye may be interested in this."

"Okay" Amy says. "Dave's here. So, tell us what the snowman is."

"Have patience," Ránulf says. He gets out of his chair and walks over to a table. "There was once a very powerful, yet very secret,'Satanic' cult here in the city. I'm sure there still are. I even know of a few. But, these were not real Satanists. These people killed mercilessly. Sacrifice after sacrifice was performed in their secret, evil temple."

"Aren't sacrifices a part of Satanism?" Amy asks.

"Nay," Ránulf says and looks at her. "Satanists do not harm living creatures, unless the creature means them harm. As I said, these people weren't Satanists. They thought they were but what they really were was a congregation of misled Christian devil worshippers."

"Isn't that the same thing?" Amy asks.

"Oh, no," Ránulf says. "Satanism is a self-indulgent religion using the Christian deity, Satan, as a symbol to perfect yourself and eventually cheat death.'Set Satanism' focuses on the Egyptian deity, Set, the god of night, darkness, and the isolated psyche. Setians set themselves as apart from nature and take godly responsibility unto themselves. But these were people who worshipped the Christian deity, Lucifer. Ease off, now, it's all part o' the tale.

"The night in question was the winter solstice of 1977. The cult had sacrificed twelve children, all under thirteen, to their deity. That night, they had to slay an infant that belonged to one of their own. The most convenient child to be sacrificed belonged to a 19-year-old cult member. She was told that her baby was to be 'baptized'. The cult's leader, Jacob Allander, took the baby and placed it on the altar. The young lass was led aside. Allander strapped the infant to the altar with straps made of human skin. He was preparing to summon the physical form of the Christian devil. He was so nervous that he did not strip the baby. That's when the mother determined it wasn't a baptism. She screamed and ran to the altar. Allander confronted her and plunged his ritual dagger into her stomach. She fell. He went back to the altar and opened the baby's coat and cut open its shirt. In the process, the infant's hat was knocked to the floor. It was an off-white color at the time. Allander called Satan in every name and language he could and then, as horrific it is to tell this, he descended the dagger into the infant. His eyes rolled to the whites and he let his robe drop to the floor. He stood there, naked and vibrating in a state of ecstasy. He didn't hear the police storm in or the gunshot that pierced his left lung. His scream was unholy as he grabbed the baby. Then, he and the baby fell to the floor, dead. However, the baby's mother was not quite dead yet. She crawled over and tried to stop the baby from bleeding by pressing his hat to the wound, soaking it. Then, as the police were occupied with the remaining cult members, she crawled out into the snow with the hat and her child, where she died. That was thirteen years ago. The winter solstice. December 21 this year, Amy."

Ránulf looks at her as her face pales.

"That's when Ricky was killed." she says with a gasp. "Three days ago."

"Wow," Dave quietly says, dumbfounded. "How do you know all that?"

"I was the one who tipped the authorities," he says. "Unfortunately it was too late. Whatever information I didn't get from the papers, I got from insiders of the cult."

"If we destroy the hat," Amy asks, "will the snowman die?"

"Aye," Ránulf answers. "If ye can get the hat, I can help with that."

"Whose soul is in the hat?" Dave asks.

"I'd wager it's Jacob Allander," Ránulf says. "He didn't know me at first, but it's been 13 years since he's seen me. After I defeated it… him… I'm sure he knew only I could wield such magic."

"What do you mean 'defeated it'?" Amy asks.

"Oh!" Ránulf gasps. "Yes, I paid a visit to your snowman."

"Is that why your shoulder was bandaged last night?" Dave asks.

Ránulf looks at the floor and sighs, "Aye, it is bandaged, still." He takes off his over-robe, leaving himself in a plain, grey, less-baggy robe.

If a robe had sweatpants, Dave thought.

His left shoulder was still bandaged. "It's healing quite well, nothing to worry about."

"What happened?" Amy asks.

"I stopped it from killing two children," Ránulf says. "But it was more powerful than I expected. I was only able to contain it, or stun it, not kill it. Near as makes n' matter, we'll have to get it back in snowman form."

Chapter 23

Rowena is busy downstairs in the shop. Two customers, both women, are browsing through the books. A man is studying the crystals and stones. Another man is talking to Rowena in the herbal area.

"Are you sure that's all you want for the mandrake?" he asks.

"Why, of course," Rowena says. "It's not imported. We grow it ourselves in our herb gardens." He pays for it and leaves. The man who was looking at the crystals buys a black onyx ring and a chunk of rose quartz. One of the women leaves without buying anything. The other woman comes to the counter with *Faerie Tale* by Raymond E. Feist and *Catmagic* by Whitley Strieber.

"Just these two, today, Rowena." She smiles.

"Some light fiction today, Carol?" Rowena smiles in return. "That will be $12.55 including tax."

"Damn," Carol frowns. "Don't you just hate that five and a half percent on top of everything?"

"Oh, there's enough hate in the world," Rowena says. "Why should I hate tax when there's millions of other people who hate it for me? Besides, it hasn't gone up since 1978 for the city, 1967 for the state."

Carol's eyebrows raise and she hands Rowena the exact change.

"I wish I was as optimistic as you, Rowena," she says.

They say goodbye and Carol leaves. Rowena pushes a button near the cash register that says "Monitor". She goes behind the curtain and takes a lemon yogurt from the fridge. She sits on the couch and begins to eat.

Then, she hears a small beep and sees a small light blinking near the curtain.

"Customer..." she grumbles as she sets her yogurt down and walks back into the store. The "Monitor" light by the register is blinking and she resets it. She frowns. No one is in the store.

Suddenly the front window shatters. She ducks behind the counter and screams. She reaches for a button that says "Alarm" next to the monitor button. Before she presses it, she hears him.

"Rowena, don't touch that, my love." The iceman stands outside the broken window frame.

"Oh, Goddess," Rowena gasps. "Be gone you foul manifestation of evil!" She stands, pointing at him. She widens her stance and raises her other arm in a Vitruvian pose. "By the Gods of the Craft, banish this blasphemic incarnation that shan't exist!"

"Oh, the showmanship!" the iceman exclaims, then growls. "Stop your charades. Your banishments and sorceries were never a match for mine."

Her face pales. "Jacob?" she barely manages to speak. "Ránulf was right!"

"Oh?" the iceman wonders. "So Rán-shitstain figured me out, did he?" Rowena tries for the alarm button but stops as the whole panel of switches becomes coated in ice. "Monitor", "Alarm", "Intercom", "1", "2", "3", "4", "5", "Lock", "Light", "Sign" and others are trapped under ice about an inch thick. She runs for the curtain which suddenly is also blocked by a wall of ice.

"That's impossible," she cries helplessly.

"I thought you were a witch," the iceman taunts. "Surely a witch would believe in the impossible." She spreads her arms and whispers "Ránulf" with urgency.

"No!" the iceman gestures at her and a thin sheet layer of ice begins to form on her body. "I don't want that old bastard interfering yet!" Rowena keels over, shivering.

"Stop it!" she screams. The iceman holds out his hand. In it, is the obsidian sphere Ránulf used to "freeze" the iceman before.

"Why don't you give this back to your old man, Rowena? I'd appreciate it." The ball floats through the window. Then it bolts toward Rowena and shoots through her forehead into her brain. Her death scream cuts abruptly short.

Chapter 24

Ránulf suddenly tilts his head upward, as if listening. He takes his staff from where it was leaning against the wall.

"What is it?" Amy asks.

"I thought I heard Rowena," he says. "I'd better go down." Dave and Amy give each other troubled glances. "I'll lead the way," Ránulf says, moving past them.

They descend the staircase with Ránulf in the lead. When they reach the bottom, Amy gasps and Ránulf's face pales. The curtained doorway to the store is blocked with ice.

"Stand back," Ránulf commands. He outstretches his arms and legs and begins to move his arms in hypnotic gestures of somatic spellcasting. Barely audible, strange verses can be heard emanating from Ránulf. Then, Amy and Dave observe in wonder as Ránulf's hands glow red. He approaches the ice and places his hands on it. Suddenly, steam erupts from contact and vision is blocked in the room. The steam surrounds everything like a thick fog. When it clears, Dave can just see Ránulf swaying as if about to faint. Dave grasps him to provide support. The ice wall is gone.

"Are you okay?" Dave asks.

"Just weak," he says. "That spell may not've looked like much, but it takes a lot out of ye."

The three of them enter the store. Everything is covered in a sheet of ice.

"Christ," Dave says. Ránulf's face is ashen.

"How?" Amy looks at him.

"I don't know..." Ránulf whispers.

"Can you dispel this, Ránulf?" Dave asks.

"No," he says. "But, Allander could never do this before. Not even anything close."

Amy screams. Dave runs to her, sliding on the icy floor, and chokes back a sob. Ránulf carefully hurries over where they see the body of Rowena beneath a sheet of ice, the obsidian sphere encrusted into the center of her forehead.

Dave and Amy simultaneously burst into tears.

Rowena shatters out of the ice and grabs Dave who utters the highest-pitched scream of his life, so far.

"I'll tear out your heart and feed it to the devil!!" she screams. Ránulf tries to pull Dave away. Rowena's eyes horrifically boil and glow. Dave manages to pull away and punches her in the jaw, breaking the lower half away from her face.

"Enough!" Ránulf screams. He puts his right hand in the horns gesture and supports himself with his staff. He points his horned fingers at Rowena. "May the Horned One of the Forest, Cernnunos, and all his forms allow the body of Rowena to at last rest in death." His hand glows a slight indigo blue.

Rowena's eyes clear and she begins to cry. Then, she falls to the ice-covered floor.

"Is she dead?" Amy cries, hysterical.

"Yes." Ránulf walks to the broken window. Amazingly, Farnum Street is empty. He wonders if the abomination of Jacob Allander killed anyone who might have otherwise been onlookers. He also wonders if the shipment of books from the distributor will be in today. He tries to wonder about anything except what Rowena must have gone through.

Dave and Amy don't miss the tears on Ránulf's face, disappearing into his beard.

"This place is no longer safe," he says. "I will summon a companion of mine to... *clean* the Covenstead, but we must go."

"Where?" Amy asks.

"Ye cannot think," he says,"that I confine myself to this dreary apartment upstairs. I set up shop here in support of Rowena. I don't know what will become of it now."

They go upstairs and Ránulf takes a few things from his library.

"Your car will be safe, here, Dave," he says. "We'll take mine."

"You have a car?" Dave asks, innocently.

"'Course I've a car," Ránulf says, raising a brow. "What sort o' daft question is that?"

"Oh nothing," Dave says quickly. "You just don't seem like you'd have a car, that's all."

"Hmph," Ránulf mutters.

They go out a door in the back and stop in front of a black Suburban.

"Where's it at?" Amy asks.

"Yeah," Dave laughs. "It's probably a hearse."

Ránulf gives Dave one of his famous dirty looks. Amy waited for Dave to be henceforth transformed into a toad. When Ránulf didn't do anything to Dave, she looked at the black Suburban and gasped. Only then did she and Dave notice the black curtains on the rear, side windows and the pewter-colored hood ornament which was a hand holding a crystal.

"Well," Dave says, "this must be yours."

They get in and drive off.

Chapter 25

Two old women are bundled up on the front screen-porch of an older-looking home. They are drinking hot tea. Their conversation ranges from sex to the weather.

"God," says Megan as she adjusts her padded bra. "This is one helluva, helluva winter, Eileen."

"I know, Meg," Eileen says. "We should've seen a thaw about now—before the worst hits."

"Why, you are right, Eileen... you are right," says Megan enthusiastically. She sips her tea.

"Meg?" asks Eileen, pausing.

"Why... yes?" urges Megan.

"Is that a padded bra you're wearing?"

Megan's wrinkled face turns bright red as she exclaims, "Well, I never!"

Suddenly, the screen of the porch is torn from its frame.

"Well, I HAVE!" shouts the iceman.

Eileen screams. Megan grabs her own chest.

"My heart… oh my heart..." she gasps. Her face is purple.

"I'm surprised you can even feel your heart through that fucken bra," the iceman snickers. "What did you pad it with? Fucking pillows?"

Megan collapses onto her chest.

"At least there was something to cushion her fall," the iceman mutters.

Eileen is sitting in her chair, petrified with terror and disbelief. The iceman steps in front of her with his arms outstretched. The whole porch becomes a blizzard of blinding snow and wind. It subsides and the iceman steps back from the women. Eileen, Megan, and everything on the porch is buried under ice and snow. The iceman chuckles. He clenches his fist and runs it through the barely alive ice-statue of Eileen. Ice breaks and blood flows.

Chapter 26

Ránulf's Suburban is moving up a long, gravel driveway lined on both sides with evergreen trees. He rolls down his window.

"Mmm," he hums. "Smell that fresh pine."

Through the trees, Dave catches a glimpse of a huge, black buck. At the same time, Ránulf hits the brakes as a gray cat flashes across the drive in front of the SUV. Amy and Dave jerk. He resumes driving.

"What was that?" Dave asks.

"It was just Bast," Ránulf answers. "She runs in front of me every time I come up this drive."

"Bast?" Amy asks.

"Aye." Ránulf smiles. "She's my cat."

"Do we get to meet your loyal familiar?" Dave asks with a smile.

Ránulf scowls at Dave.

"Ye hath a very sarcastic personality," Ránulf scolds, raising his eyebrows. "And ye'd better lose it if around me for a while. Which ye are."

"Until spring," Amy mutters.

"Umm," Dave starts. "Like, I have to be home by dark tonight. Unless… Ránulf here mesmerizes my parents or something."

Ránulf frowns. "I do not 'mesmerize' the parents of smart ass lads. Ye'll have to deal with the punishment after this is over."

They come out of the trees and see a large limestone house resembling a small castle. A large forest looms behind it and rolling, snow-covered hills trail off on either side. Amy inhales a surprised breath of awe.

"You live here?" Dave asks in wonder.

"Sometimes," Ránulf answers. They drive into a small, gravel parking area and exit the vehicle. A gray cat runs toward them and leaps, almost floating, onto Ránulf's shoulder.

"Merry meet, Bast," Ránulf greets her. Bast looks at Dave and Amy, then questionably meows at Ránulf. Ránulf's face saddens. "I am sorry, Bast, but..." He looks at Dave and Amy, then takes Bast in his arms. He turns his back to the couple. Dave and Amy look at each other, confused. They hear Ránulf conversing with Bast but not in any human language. Only the familiar sounds of two cats. Then, Bast leaps out of Ránulf's arms and runs off, scattering snow in her wake.

"What was that all about?" Dave asks.

"She wanted to know where Rowena was," Ránulf quietly answers.

Chapter 27

Later, Ránulf, Dave, and Amy are sitting at a table drinking hot chocolate. Dave is browsing through *Complete Book of Witchcraft* which Ránulf lent him from the Covenstead.

"Is this place left alone when you're away?" asks Amy.

"Oh, nay," answers Ránulf. "Two dear friends of mine look after the house and the villagers look after the estate."

Dave looks up from the book. "What villagers?"

"Oh," Ránulf remarks and takes a sip of his cocoa. "Just a small group of Wiccans and a couple other groups of neopagans. They tend to a small but self-sufficient village and farm on the estate." Just then a door slams. Footfall can be heard approaching the door to the room. Ránulf gets to his feet.

A young, clean-shaven man with long, blonde hair enters with a young, black-haired woman. They both wear homespun robes of black.

"Theena! Rowan! Greetings!" Ránulf bellows.

"Well met, Ránulf," Rowan replies, smiling and putting his arm around Theena.

"Hello, Ránulf," Theena says.

"Theena, Rowan," he gestures at Dave and Amy. "This is Dave and that is Amy."

"Hi," Dave and Amy say together.

"They will be guests here for a while," Ránulf announces. "Theena, will ye please show them to their… *separate* rooms?" Dave laughs. Amy blushes. Theena leads them upstairs. Dave carries his book and a bag he brought from his car the prior night at the bookstore.

Ránulf is left alone with Rowan.

"What's the story with them?" Rowan asks.

"Ye are as impatient as they are." Ránulf laughs a harsh laugh. "Do ye remember Jacob Allander?"

"Ye mean that old misled Christian devil worshipper?" mimics Rowan.

"Aye." Ránulf sighs. "But alas, his soul did not perish along with his body."

Ránulf begins to tell Rowan the story, starting with what Amy and Dave told him and stopping when he gets to the part where he faced the ice blocking the curtained way into the shop.

"Well…" Rowan rubs his eyes. "Then what?"

"I used a method of a *Dispelling Cold* spell to get rid of the ice," Ránulf says. "Then we went into the store. It was all… ice."

"What about my mother?" Rowan's face pales.

"Rowan... I…" Ránulf looks away.

"Ránulf, please..." Rowan begs, almost in tears. Ránulf looks at Rowan. His eyes seem to say "please don't make me say this" and he begins to cry. "Rowena is dead."

Rowan loses his color until his skin almost matches his hair. "No," he manages to whisper. Ránulf embraces him.

"I've sent Geoff to get her," Ránulf says. "Tomorrow night, she'll be given a decent pagan burial here on the estate."

"Oh gods," Rowan cries. He pulls away from the wizard. "I-I should be happy," he cries. "Sh-she's with the gods, now." Rowan manages a hurt smile.

Theena enters and looks from Rowan to Ránulf.

"What?" she asks. A pause.

"Rowena... has passed over," Ránulf says.

"Ah... Goddess," Theena whispers. She goes to Rowan with an embrace.

Chapter 28

Dave is in his room. He is wearing a robe which looks similar to Rowan's. The room is warm and peaceful. There is a dresser, a bed, two cushioned armchairs, and a bureau with a mirror and water basin on it. He looks at all this and laughs, amused by the antiquity of it. He leaves the room to walk down the hall a small way with his headphones on and then stops. He removes the headphones.

"Fuck," he mutters as he takes the cassette tape out of the player, stretching and unspooling the exposed tape. "Shit. It ate my King Diamond tape." The door he is in front of opens and Amy steps out, wearing another one of the grey robes.

"Hey guttermouth," she teases. Dave joins her in her room. He leaves his headphones and his *The Eye* cassette on a nightstand in the hall.

Between kisses, Dave notices Amy's room is much like his own, except with a feminine touch. Where his room was a bit utilitarian, she had a canopied bed. They slip between the curtains onto it and Dave's hand slips inside of Amy's robe. The fact that she's not wearing a bra makes his flesh all the stiffer. She unties her robe exposing her slightly pink flesh and her white panties. Dave's hand slips into those white panties and she stops kissing him to catch her breath. She unties Dave's robe as Dave amateurly fondles the contours of her breasts. She runs her tongue down Dave's chest, wetting the newly-born hair most eighteen year olds are proud of. She can't help but notice Dave's erected gland protruding from the waistline of his Hanes Classic underwear. She grasps it and begins to stroke, receiving nothing but pleasant groans from Dave. Dave lies on his back as Amy sits on his chest, her back facing his face. She pushes his underpants to his ankles and begins to massage his balls and impressive mass of pubic hair. She bends over slowly and places her mouth over the tip of Dave's erection. His breathing speeds up and she can just barely feel his heart beating quite rapidly beneath her rear. She engulfs Dave's rod with her mouth and gasps as one of Dave's fingers probes her labia. There is a knock at Amy's door.

"Amy?" questions Theena's voice. Amy retreats from her perch and ties her robe. Theena opens the door and gasps.

Dave pulls up his Hanes, gets off the bed, and quickly starts to tie his robe. As his erection begins to subside, a damp spot of precum forms on his underwear.

"I thought this might be where you were." She looks at Dave, a smile hinting on her face as she glances at his pelvis. "Amy, Ránulf wishes to speak with you in the library. Follow me." She walks out the door and Amy follows, face beet-red. Theena turns around.

"Oh Dave," she says. "Rowan also needs to talk to you. He's in your room." Theena and Amy walk down the hall and descend the stairs. Dave grabs his headphones and tape as he heads to his room.

Rowan is on Dave's bed looking through Dave's bag and the cassettes he packed. Alice in Chains' *Facelift* and Black Sabbath's *TYR* cassettes are laying out on the bed. Dave is surprised to find that he harbors no resentment toward Rowan's unwarranted search through his belongings.

"Hi," Dave says as his eyes meet Rowan's.

"Hello, David," Rowan replies, cheerily.

"Your umm... wife? She said you wanted to talk to me," Dave says.

"Oh," Rowan says. "Theena is not my wife. The gods know she wants to handfast with me but I keep telling her that 20 is too young to be married."

Then Dave notices a black electric guitar in the corner.

"My guitar!" he exclaims.

"Aye, as Ránulf would say," Rowan jokes. "Geoff brought it from your house." Dave picks it up.

"How?" he asks.

"Well," Rowan says, "Ránulf called your parents and found out your recent history. You know, just barely graduating from school, no desire for college, et cetera, et cetera."

"Yeah?" Dave asks.

"Well, Ránulf told them he would privately school you in common college courses. Even though he'll school you in a few more uncommon courses, too. *If* you know what I mean. Ránulf is perfectly capable of teaching almost any subject, too."

Dave laughs.

"What's funny?" Rowan asks, surprised.

"I'm trying to picture Ránulf talking on a phone," Dave laughs again. Rowan joins him.

"So, I'm here for good?" Dave asks.

"Or for bad, yes." Rowan smirks.

"I can handle that," Dave replies with a smile.

"Geoff can take you home tomorrow, for *Christmas*." Rowan pronounces "Christmas" bitterly. "Then you can get the rest of your stuff. By the way, Geoff also brought your car from Covenstead."

"Who's this Geoff person?" Dave asks.

"Geoff runs all our errands and does the estate's dirty work. Oh, and don't worry about anything... he's loyal and a friend. Not only is he a witch, he's the only one of us around that's a martial artist, too."

Dave nods, taking it in. "A real manwitch." Then he changes to the subject he'd been wondering about. "Did Ránulf teach you?"

"Ránulf is still teaching me." Rowan raises his eyebrows, sighs, and stands up. "But now, I fear Theena has evening-feast ready and you should meet our *manwitch*."

Rowan and Dave leave the room. As they get to the stairs, a hand falls on Dave's shoulder. He yelps and his face pales. He turns to face Ránulf.

"Ránulf?" Dave asks, to be sure.

"Aye," Ránulf says.

"You'll get used to the old mage sneaking up on 'ye', Dave," Rowan jests. He and Dave laugh. Ránulf scowls.

"Truly amazing how similar ye two are," Ránulf says but it just gets Dave and Rowan laughing again.

"Ye should be serious, David," Ránulf says. "Ye'd best give Amy some space or ye'll be sleeping down in the village. Then ye'll be frolicking unclad with purpose instead of lust."

They all three descend the staircase. Theena, Amy, and a man are already at the table. The man looks about 28 and has short, black hair.

Ránulf gestures at him. "Dave, this is Geoff and vice versa. Now that everyone knows each other, let's eat."

Ránulf and the others sit down and begin eating the wonderful meal Theena prepared.

Chapter 29

After dinner, they all retire to their chambers except Rowan and Geoff who are on dish duty. Dave goes into his room and falls asleep right after his head hits the pillow. Amy lies awake, thinking of what Ránulf had told her.

"Ye're going to run the new bookshop, Amy," he had said. "Ye can live upstairs like Rowena and I used to do. I haven't found a living companion for ye, yet—"

"What about Dave?" she had interrupted.

"David will begin his studies here, with me," he paused. "So I can keep both eyes on him." He stopped. There had been scratching at the door. Amy's gaze grew fearful. Ránulf merely smiled. Theena, who was in the back kitchen with them, had opened the door. Amy actually saw the snowman kill Theena. In her mind, it buried its hatchet blade in her skull.

But then she got control of herself. She may have seen the snowman for a terrifying, split second but what really bounded in was a gorgeous timber wolf. She jumped in her seat.

"Timbre!" exclaimed Theena as she bent over and nuzzled the wolf.

"That is Theena's familiar," Ránulf had informed her.

"She has a wolf… and you have a *cat*?" Amy asked, incredulously..

"Bast is the familiar of all witches on the estate." Ránulf smiled. "I have a more exotic familiar. At least, I've seen nowt else communicating with an obsidian black buck, of late."

"What's Rowan's familiar?" Amy had asked.

"Rowan has the honor of an unkindness of ravens," Theena had said. Timbre sniffed Amy and locked her innocent, yet cunning, eyes with Amy's eyes.

Amy smiles at this recollection as she lies awake in bed. Imagine a life with these animals at this manor. And the thrill of ever seeing the witch village, hidden somewhere on the estate. Away from the confining and choking city... she began to cry. Her little brother and parents were dead. All killed by a snowman. *I must be going insane*, thinks Amy. Then her window blows open, the cold air lifting the curtains of her canopied bed like a pale pink spectre reaching for her soul. Amy utters a cry of alarm. She gets out of bed to shut the window but what to her wondering eyes should appear?

A miniature snowman and eight dead reindeer. The prancing and tapping of each little hoof stopped forever when they fell off the roof. The driver, his features so icy, so slick… she knew right that moment it wasn't St. Nick!

"Tomorrow's Christmas, Amy." The snowman grins from the snow-covered lawn. "I'll be waiting."

A cat suddenly jumps onto the window sash. Amy starts to scream but realizes it is Bast. "Bast," Amy says with a gasp.

The familiar seems to greet her in her mind. Amy looks out the window. The snowman and the eight, dead reindeer are gone but the tracks in the snow are clear enough.

What have you gotten us into? the cat's eyes seem to ask. *The village and covenstead have been in danger before but never from the supernatural. Nothing beyond the ability of Ránulf and us familiars to face.*

Below the second story window, Amy sees Timbre watching her. Rowan's ravens can be seen in the bare trees and just on the horizon, Amy can make out the form of a black buck.

Beware, the end is coming, Bast`s eyes say to Amy. *But will it be for the snowman or for us?*

The cat departs. The ravens fly off. The wolf bounds across the yard and out of sight. The buck has vanished.

Amy closes her window.

Chapter 30

Dave is asleep… or is he? Now, he's walking down the stairs. He walks into the kitchen then into a back room off the kitchen for food prep and storage. He hears scratching at a door to the outside. Slowly, he walks over to the door and opens it. The snowman pushes in wielding his ax.

"Hello, Davey-boy," he screams. "Remember me?"

"Holy shit—" Dave cries in surprise. The snowman pushes past him into the room, leaving Dave standing there looking stupid. Dave hears Amy scream.

"Amy?" Dave whispers. "NO!" he screams. He bolts up the stairs and into… Ránulf's room? Ránulf is there, seated in his chair, and the snowman brings the ax down into his face. Blood gushes everywhere. Dave screams. He runs to the next door and throws it open, then sees Theena lying dead on the floor and the snowman killing Rowan.

Dave runs to the next room. A frigid wind from the open window blows the curtains of a pale-pink canopied bed. Dave cautiously walks up to the bed and parts the curtains.

"Amy?" he whispers. She rolls over and yawns.

"Dave?" she asks. Dave lets out a sigh of relief.

Suddenly, the bed curtains on the opposite side blow open and the snowman rises from the floor, swinging his ax.

"Say goodbye to your bitch, Dave," the snowman cackles. Amy screams, gurgles, and dies as the snowman brings the ax down into her breasts. The snowman smiles at Dave who staggers back… and faints.

Chapter 31

Dave wakes up in his own bed. "Oh... fuck..." he mutters. "I have one big bastard of a headache." Geoff, who was waiting for him to awaken, walks to the side of the bed.

"Theena will have something for that, I'd bet," he says.

"Geoff?" Dave looks confused.

Geoff lays some clothes on Dave's bed. "Your mother gave me a bunch of your clothes," he explains. "We'll go get the rest after you get dressed and eat. Breakfast?"

"Breakfast?" Dave asks. "At least you didn't say 'morning feast!'"

Geoff smiles and leaves.

Then Dave remembers. *But Theena's dead... Ránulf too! And...* "Oh God!" He cries out and quickly slips into fresh socks and underwear, a Slayer t-shirt, and black jeans. He runs to Amy's door and knocks. No answer. He opens the door, goes over to the bed, and quietly opens the curtains. Bast is lying asleep on Amy's pillow. She raises her head and looks into Dave's eyes, her stare containing secrets and absolutely no sense of humor.

Theena walks into the room.

"Dave?" she asks. He jumps.

"Geoff said you had a 'big bastard' of a headache, so I made this." She holds a steaming cup of tea out to him. He takes it, his hands shaking.

Dave takes a sip and looks back at the bed—Bast is gone. The window is shut.

"Dave," Theena asks, "what's wrong?"

"I..." He pauses. "I guess it was just a dream, that's all."

Dave drinks the tea. "Thanks," he says. "I feel better already."

They go downstairs. Geoff serves Rowan, Theena, and Dave. Amy and Ránulf are absent from the table, so Dave asks their whereabouts.

"Ránulf took Amy on a small tour of the village," Rowan says.

Dave pales.

"Oh, don't worry," Theena says. "They'll be around other witches the whole time. They're perfectly safe." Dave resumes eating.

After they finish, Geoff agrees to drive Dave home to get the belongings he'll need for his move into the manor. They get into a black pickup truck and drive off down the driveway. Bast and Timbre watch them depart, then take off running over a field behind the house.

Meanwhile, Theena and Rowan are in a common living room, making out on a couch. Rowan's robe is tied around his waist, leaving him bare from the waist up. Theena's robe is untied, revealing she's wearing nothing beneath it. Rowan massages her mound with his hand.

"Shit," Rowan mutters as he pulls his mouth away from Theena's, "I should've started the fire." He gets up and walks over to the fireplace, which is already set up. He strikes a long match to light it. It blazes instantly, sending heat throughout the room. Rowan rejoins Theena on the couch. She lets her robe fall and then she removes Rowan's. Rowan kisses her breasts and nipples while Theena tickles his balls with her fingernails. Soon his shaft is fully erect. Slowly, Theena mounts him, rocking back and forth. Their breathing grows heavier as they speed up. Theena climaxes with a cry, then Rowan shoots his load into her confines, groaning. He withdraws and lies spent on the couch, Theena on top of him.

Smoke emanates from the mansion's chimney. Over the rim of

the chimney, an ice-hand appears. Its withered fingers snap as it attempts to clutch the edge. Another hand appears and barely grabs the rim. A thin, partially-melted iceman emerges. "Goddammit!" he cries. "They started the fucking fire." He flies from the roof to shatter into the snow below. Then two sticks from under a nearby tree slide along the snow toward the hat that remains. The snowman reforms where the iceman had shattered. It touches its face—coal eyes, carrot nose, chocolate-chip mouth. "Good fucking deal," he mutters. "Didn't even have to go find my facial features."

In the kitchen, Theena is washing dishes. Rowan comes up behind to join her. A black cat runs through the kitchen.

"Who?" Theena asks.

"It wasn't Bast," Rowan observes. "Probably a cat from the village. I'll go after it."

Rowan leaves Theena alone to finish washing dishes in front of a pane-glass window. Some suds splash onto the window, and she reaches to wipe them off—just as the glass shatters. She screams. The snowman's stick-arm wraps around her wrist.

"Oh shit," she says. She breaks the stick-arm against a cupboard and rushes to the back door. She yells back into the house for Rowan and quickly dons her boots before bursting out into the snow. "Where are you, bastard?" she demands. She tries to take a step but finds her boots frozen in ice beneath her. She stretches out her arms. "Timbre," she whispers, "Timbre, Timbre!" Then a snowball hits her in the face. She hears the snowman's laughter.

Chapter 32

Elsewhere, Ránulf is pointing to huts and small cabins from a small hill. "That's the village?" Amy asks. "I didn't know the covenstead was so huge—" They hear a wolf howl as Timbre and Bast run up to them. Timbre stops, cocks her head to listen, then howls again. She looks at Ránulf, then bounds off. Bast meets Ránulf's gaze—her eyes say it all: *It's here.*

"Damn," he mutters, then begins to walk toward the village. "The village is closer. We keep a snowmobile there for emergencies." He looks at Bast and says, "Bring it." She bounds off toward the village. Ránulf raises his hands and begins to hum, knowing from Timbre's behavior that Theena was in need of urgent aid. He envisions a protective sphere of white light around Theena, knowing it won't help for long. He quickly looks toward the direction of the village and utters a series of low, gurgling croaks, harsh grating sounds, and a sharp, raspy bird call. From the village, where they were being fed, the black ravens take flight, believing Rowan has summoned them. The children who were feeding the birds know this must mean trouble and scurry off to tell their mothers.

Bast reaches the village, howling. A man runs to her in surprise. "Bast?" In his mind flash images of himself rushing in the snowmobile to collect Ránulf and Amy. A glimpse of the future just about to happen. He opens the double-wide doors of a nearby storage shack and gets the snowmobile running. He sets off, Bast leading the way.

While reinforcements gather, Theena is outside, armed with a homemade javelin she'd left by the back door since their winter solstice celebration. The snowman sees an ax sticking out of a tree stump on the opposite side of the house.

"How I love axes." He sneers. He pulls it out of the stump with his freshly replaced stick-arm and slides toward the back of the house.

Theena, who is barefoot, frees her boots from the ice and puts them on.

"So, who might you be, young lass?" he taunts. "I usually know everyone's name off the top of my snowy head but Ránulf seems to have cast a protection spell on you. Too bad it won't actually protect you." It swings the ax, but Theena deflects it with her javelin, the force driving her back.

"You won't live to know my name," she threatens. She maneuvers cautiously out of the reach of his next swing, placing herself beneath a massive, snow-covered cedar tree. On his next strike, Theena disarms the snowman, causing his ax to fly several feet away. Then, an impossible load of snow falls from the tree, burying Theena.

Inside the house, Rowan is kneeling next to a couch, looking behind it. "Here, kitty, kitty. Come here." He stands up to stretch his back. The ravens begin to urgently peck at a nearby window. They squawk and try to fly through the glass.

"Shit!" Rowan exclaims. He runs to the back door and puts his boots on. He pulls a sword and belt from a cabinet, straps on the belt, and places the sword in its sheath. He runs through the door and gives a bird call identical to Ránulf's.

The ravens circle overhead and alight in the tree above Theena. Timbre sprints into view to help Theena by digging in the snow around where she is buried. Timbre whines as she uncovers

Theena's face. Rowan utters a cry of concern and rushes over to lift an unconscious Theena from the snow. The snowman begins to slide slowly toward Rowan. Timbre snarls and the ravens noisily take to the air.

Rowan's eyes widen, not knowing how to get Theena safely inside while also avoiding an attack. Sensing her opportunity, Timbre lunges at the snowman, getting a mouthful of nothing but snow which melts into blood in her mouth. The snowman swings his ax at Timbre and misses. The ravens flock around the snowman, blocking his view of and access to Rowan and Theena.

Rowan carries Theena inside and places her on the couch. He goes after some herbs, salve, and a wet cloth. He also returns with an unguent that he places under Theena's nose. She begins to awaken.

Outside, the snowman swings at Timbre and grazes her back with his ax. She yelps and collapses. He spins around and splits a raven in half as the others flee into the sky. The snowman leaps into the house, in pursuit of Rowan and Theena.

"Damn, it is *warm* in here!" The snowman enters the kitchen and forms a snowball in his stick-hand. He throws it against the far wall where it explodes and covers the entire kitchen in snow.

Outside, Ránulf, Amy, and Bast finally arrive in the snowmobile and race to the backyard. Bast leaps to Timbre's side while Amy runs inside and gasps.

"The kitchen is frozen!" she calls out to Ránulf. He pushes in past her and raises his staff.

Down the hall in the next room, the snowman slides toward Rowan. "Can you protect yourself and your beloved?" he asks. He aims his charcoal gaze toward the burning fireplace and it freezes over.

The snowman swings his ax at Rowan who intercepts it with his sword. Rowan presses forward but, surprised at the strength of the stick-arms, he is unable to dislodge the ax from the snowman's grip. The snowman begins to utter an unnerving laugh as it begins to snow in the room.

Theena awakens and discreetly sits up from the couch. She raises a couch cushion and approaches from behind the snowman. Rowan, in his fear, betrays her with a glance in her direction and the snowman spins around to swing his ax at her. It lands square center in the cushion, splitting into the stuffing.

Rowan slices off part of the snowman's head with his sword. Blood suddenly soaks the snowman, spreading from the "wound". The snowman pulls his ax free of the cushion and leaps at Theena, but suddenly Ránulf's staff knocks another part of its face off, sending a spray of snow everywhere—a coal eye falls to the floor.

"Hello, Jacob," Ránulf greets the snowman. "I was wondering when ye'd show." He knocks the snowman's ax away with his staff, then raises his arms and utters an unknowable word.

The snowfall stops and the snowman shrieks as if in pain.

Theena retreats to where Amy is watching at the edge of the room. Ránulf moves his hand in a quick pattern and sends three electric-blue daggers of light jetting toward the snowman.

They plunge into his snow-body, but the snowman recovers. He slashes Rowan's face with a stick-arm. Rowan cries out.

Ránulf's staff strikes again and snags on the snowman's hat.

"You son of a bitch," the snowman growls. But the hat won't come off of his head, almost as if it's frozen on. The snowman raises his stick-arms and the snow on the floor whirls around Ránulf, freezing him in a roundish case of ice.

"No..." Rowan cries in horror.

Bast's eyes grow wide. She howls and attacks the snowman, biting off half his carrot-nose.

"I hate cats!" the snowman bellows, chopping at Bast. He misses just as Rowan lands another blow with his sword to his head, trying to dislodge the hat. The snowman howls and leaps through the window, shattering both the glass and itself. Amy chases after and peeks outside. The snowman is gone, hat and all. Rowan and Theena stare in awe at the ice case that still encloses Ránulf.

"How are we going to get him out of this?" Theena asks. Rowan's face appears to finally have given way to shock.

Amy sucks in a breath, realizing what she nearly forgot. "Theena! Timbre is out back, hurt!" Theena leaves to attend to her familiar.

"Ránulf?" Rowan asks. His closed eyes do not move under the ice. Amy starts to get a fire going again in the hearth.

"Rowan… it's too wet and icy to start a fire." Her eyes tear up in frustration as he rushes from the room.

Rowan leafs through Ránulf's library for a spell and finds notes on a variation of a *Dispelling Cold* incantation tucked into *Weather Manipulation*. He takes the note and rushes back to Amy and Ránulf.

"Maybe stand back, Amy," he cautions. "I've only had a little practice with this kind of… sorcery." He stands in front of Ránulf and briefly studies the note. He sticks it in his belt and begins to chant. He moves his hands similar to the motion Ránulf had made earlier. A slight fiery aura surrounds Rowan's hands. He faces his palms outward toward Ránulf and utters a word in a language Amy could not decipher.

The ice melts—along with Ránulf himself, who dissolves into a puddle on the floor.

"No," Rowan whispers in disbelief. Amy cries out in a panic. Theena is at the threshold of the room having witnessed the horror, Timbre in her arms. She lies Timbre on the couch.

"Rowan?" she starts.

"I don't know what happened!"

"He's dead!" Amy shrieks.

"No one step in this!" Rowan commands and rushes back to Ránulf's library.

Theena kneels by the puddle. Ránulf's face briefly appears in it, then vanishes. There is nothing left. Stunned, Theena returns to Timbre's side.

Chapter 33

Rowan rifles desperately through more books. *This all feels impossible,* he thinks. *What kind of a spell in a book would even come close to bringing Ránulf back? On top of that, how would I even come close to being the one who could pull it off?* The feeling of wanting to give up clashes with the knowing he would never stop searching. Amy knocks and enters the library.

"Rowan," she hesitates. "Theena wants to check the scratch on your face."

Rowan glances at his reflection in a glass bookcase and realizes his injury will need to be cleaned and bandaged. "I didn't know it was that bad." He begins to finally cry. He pauses his search, reluctantly joins Amy, and leaves the library.

Chapter 34

Geoff and Dave have arrived at Dave's house to gather Dave's belongings. After an hour of packing, Dave stares at his blank walls while Geoff talks to his parents in another room. After a moment, his mother comes into his room.

"We're going to miss you, honey." She embraces him as he grimaces.

"I'll miss you, too, Mom."

"Geoff seems like a nice person," she says. "And I am sure Professor 'Randolph' is a good teacher." Dave hides his smile at the addition of the honorific *and* her mispronunciation.

Geoff and Dave pile into the truck and begin the drive back.

Thirty minutes later, they start up the long drive to the manor. It is starting to snow. Off the side of the road, snowmen form and dissolve along the way, toying with them.

"I thought something felt weird about this snow," Dave says.

"There is an evil energy to it," Geoff agrees. "It's in the air and I'm worried. This is where Bast usually runs by to greet me whenever I come up the drive. I haven't seen her."

"Then let's step on it," Dave encourages. Geoff speeds up.

They both gasp as they see one of the snowmen in the drive directly in their path. "Plow it!" Dave yells.

The snowman remains stationary as the truck speeds toward it and plows through it. Geoff and Dave both let out a sigh of relief, immediately followed by yells when they see another snowman blocking their path.

"What the fuck?" Geoff exclaims.

"He's playing with us!" Dave yells in anger.

Once again, Geoff speeds up and crashes through the snowman.

This time, not surprised, Geoff increases his speed as yet another snowman stands in the way. As they smash through it, a wave of blood and slush covers the truck. Dave screams. Geoff flips on the windshield wipers which only modestly help to clear their view. The truck clears the trees as they approach the final, short stretch to the house. In the road is one more giant snowman, towering 12 feet above the drive.

"Shit," Dave utters. "This one could be real."

"Why?" Geoff asks. "Because it's fucking huge?"

"It's wearing a hat," Dave whimpers.

Geoff continues to speed towards the snowman. Dave looks out the rear window at the drive behind them and the snowmen they had crashed through were all there, fully-formed and facing them. Dave quickly looks back at the giant snowman they are rapidly nearing, and sees the ax.

"Geoff! Look out!"

The massive snowman leaps onto the hood, smashing the windshield with his ax and mostly falling apart in the process. Geoff slams the brakes, but a swirling drift of snow forms in front of the truck and they skid off the drive. They slam into the drift and what's left of the snowman crumbles. Dave and Geoff get out of the truck and abandon the vehicle.

"We'll have to run for the house," Geoff says.

They start to trek uphill to the manor, making their way through the deep snow back to the driveway. They start up the drive when Geoff suddenly grabs Dave's arm, stopping him. The snowman is at the top of the hill between them and the house. Regular size again.

"Hi guys!" The snowman waves his arms at them enthusiastically. "Today… is Christmas! And boy oh boy, do I have a present for you!" The snowman begins to absorb snow from the ground around him until he becomes one, large snowball. Then, he begins to roll down the hill towards the guys.

Dave and Geoff both run in different directions, left and right of the drive while still trying to decrease the distance between themselves and the manor at the top of the hill.

The snowball rolls down the hill, growing larger, and passes through where they had been standing. They look back at it but continue to trudge up the hill. The snowball stops, although the slope should have carried it further into the tree-lined drive. It slowly begins to roll back up the hill, continuing to absorb surrounding snow. Dave and Geoff both look at it, horrified and again make a break for the house. The snowball picks up speed to match their pace, growing enormous.

Inside, Timbre and Bast's ears perk up. Theena and Amy hear shouting and rush to the front door to open it. They both gasp as they see the giant snowball, now easily rolling up the hill with somewhere between a 10-12 foot diameter. Geoff falls back to ensure he is not too far ahead of Dave. Amy stares at the scene, not knowing what to do. Theena rushes back in to alert Rowan.

"Dave!" Amy screams, hysterically. "Run!"

The edge of the snow boulder catches the edge of Dave's heel and he falls. The snowball runs him over as Theena rejoins Amy in the doorway and they both scream "Dave!"

The snowball slows as Dave surfaces at the top, almost completely buried in the snow. It comes to a stop with Dave sticking out midway on the decline, facing the house. He is gasping for air and bleeding from the head.

Rowan appears outside the manor, his eyes blazing. A silver disc engraved with runes rests in his palm as he aims it at the snowball and shouts an incantation. The giant snowball collapses, freeing Dave, who struggles to stand. Geoff pulls him to his feet and they make their way, met halfway by Theena and Amy, inside the house. An owl, watching from a tree, takes flight into the woods.

The figure of a man made of snow, with the hat and features of the snowman, steps out of the pile of the collapsed snowball. He dashes down the drive, watched from the trees by Rowan's ravens.

Chapter 35

Dave is lying on his bed at the manor. Amy and Theena are sitting at the edge, talking. He begins to stir.

"Dave?" Amy asks. "Are you ok?"

He groans and sits halfway up, leaning on his elbow. "Yeah, I'm ok now, I think. Where are Geoff and Ránulf?"

"Geoff's downstairs with Rowan in the library," Theena says, ignoring his question about Ránulf.

"We should go back to the truck and get my stuff if it's safe," Dave says. "Whatever didn't get ruined, at least."

"Rowan and Geoff got the truck unstuck and unloaded it while you were out," Amy says.

"What time is it?" he asks.

"4:00," Amy says, checking her Swatch.

Despite protests from both young women, Dave makes his way to the library. Rowan and Geoff turn to him as he enters.

"Rowan, what happened to your face?" Dave cries, concerned.

"You don't like it?" Rowan replies, bitterly. "Oh, you know, some guy wearing a hat stained with the blood of the ages and carrying an ax dropped in, had tea by the fire, fucked me up, and killed Ránulf."

"Killed Ránulf?" Dave asks in disbelief.

"The snowman froze him," Amy says, her tone measured.

"And Rowan melted him," Theena finished.

Bast waltzes back and forth across the library desk and utters an impatient *meow*. She knocks some papers to the floor, looks satisfied, then leaps down to leave the room. The remaining five of them move into the living room, where Ránulf was last seen alive. The spot on the floor where he melted, now a drying, discolored spot on the hardwoods. Amy is finally able to get a small fire going in the hearth.

Theena sits on the couch where Rowan had Christmas-dicked her that morning. She shuffles her Tarot cards. Geoff closes the shutters over the window broken earlier by the snowman's exit.

"So." Dave exhales, not realizing he had been holding in his breath. "What are we going to do?" They all look to Rowan.

"I think we can agree that we have to destroy the hat," he states. "It appears to be his anchor to our world. The question is how to get it from him."

"How did you stop the giant snowball, Rowan?" asks Amy.

"Ránulf has four silver discs," he replies. "Each bears some influence over the elements of Earth, Air, Fire, and Water. They can add some extra juice to simple spells and can be recharged on the following *Esbat*, or full moon. I remember Ránulf telling me that each can also be used once per year for a major working, giving complete control over an element. They each have a particular Sabbat associated with them where they would need to be ritually recharged if used for that purpose. I used the talisman for Water to provide enough control over the snow to cause the snowball to collapse."

"Mildly spectacular," Dave sarcastically contributes. "So we can use the disc for Fire to blow the fucker back to Hell?"

"Or I can use the one for Earth to bury you under the old Faerie mound," Rowan retorts.

"Christ took a shit, you two!" Amy emits, exhausted. "We all have a mutual problem here!"

"Aye," comes a familiar voice. "And if ye don't gi'oer with the theatrics, I won't tell ye Ránulf Wylkyn's 'Four Step Plan for Killing Snowmen'."

Ránulf walks into the room—alive.

Geoff, Theena, and Amy all call out his name. Rowan vomits into a planter, in shock or possibly even relief.

"A deception of the mind and eyes for the snowman," Ránulf explains. "An illusion as if I had melted, but I slipped away to retrieve something... This." He holds up an antiquated leather-bound tome. "The very compendium Jacob Allander used to summon that fallacious Christian god of evil and deceit—Satan.

With this, I can banish Allander back to Gehenna where he belongs."

The group debates their next steps. Ránulf tells them to go about their normal duties until the snowman shows again. "I have watchers," he says. "They'll alert me." He retrieves the other three elemental discs from a safe behind some books on a shelf in the library, thinking he may need them before they have completed their mission.

"You didn't know last time it was here," Amy reminds him.

"Ye have an intact memory," he says. "I took our wards for granted and was not expecting him to come here. I didn't think—"

"You didn't think it would come here?" Rowan angrily interrupts. "What *did* you think? That it would just forget you, Dave, and Amy and just go after more innocent kids? While you just sit out here in your castle on the hill on your mystical ass? You would have just sat here, while it went on killing, playing magic and jerking off?"

"Rowan!" Theena shouts. "Stop it!" Amy and Dave share a shocked glance.

"No, let him go on, Theena," Ránulf says, calmly. "It is good for him to get this anger out so it doesn't cloud him later. Go on, lad. Breathe deep and settle yerself. Now then, what's weighin' on thee? I dare say it was me 'jerking off'?"

Rowan scowls. His eyes and face take on a look of pure hatred. In a voice not his own, he says, "I want to see you *dead,* old man!"

All except Ránulf gasp.

He continues. "I want to see you on the ground, writhing naked in pain! I want to sever your head, amputate your arms, and eat your cock!" He reaches angrily towards Ránulf.

Geoff grabs him to hold him back and Dave rushes to assist him.

"Leave his body, Allander," Ránulf commands, looking deep into Rowan's possessed eyes.

"Never, motherfucker!" Rowan breaks free of Geoff's grip and shoves Dave away. Theena and Amy rush him and with preternatural strength, he shoves them flying to the ground. He grabs a double-edged athame from the fireplace mantle. "Now it's time for the mighty mage to finally die!" Rowan runs at Ránulf and attempts to stab him in the chest. Ránulf grabs Rowan's wrist without blinking.

"DROP IT," he commands. Rowan bellows laughter and flings Ránulf against a bookcase. Geoff tackles Rowan from behind. Rowan grunts and elbows him hard in the face. He spins around and stabs Geoff in the shoulder. Geoff screams and pulls away from Rowan, his hand going to the blade's hilt sticking out of his shoulder.

Theena delivers a roundhouse kick to Rowan's face. He slams back tripping over an end table, hitting his head on the way to the floor, unconscious. Theena gives him a once-over to make sure he's out, then rushes to tend to Geoff's wound. Dave helps Ránulf off the floor while Amy looks for something to restrain Rowan's hands and legs.

"I'll take this patient, Theena," Ránulf joins her in bringing Geoff to the couch where Theena produces her healing kit. Ránulf places a towel beneath Geoff's bleeding shoulder. "Theena, envision the proper healing auras, please." He rips Geoff's shirt sleeve to provide access to the wound and begins to put an ointment around the protruding knife. Theena envisions a blue aura around Geoff and his wound. She pictures the wound closed, healed, and the bleeding stopped. She imbues her intentions into the blue light, disinfecting, styptic, and healing.

Ránulf begins to grasp the knife, gauze ready in his other hand. "Geoff, talk to me."

"The numbing ointment is shit," he grunts.

Ránulf reaches into the kit and prepares a syringe.

"No," Geoff says. "If it isn't herbal, I can take the pain."

"Oh, it is all natural." Ránulf winks at him. "Though, if it were chemical,'twould numb ye more. This will do, this will do." He locates the necessary anatomical landmarks and injects the needle posterolaterally between Dave's neck and shoulder. "This should help with the bleeding, too."

"Ránulf," Theena cautions. "That will knock him out."

"It could kill him," he counters. "If we don't hurry." He grasps the handle and withdraws the blade. Blood spurts from the wound. He quickly applies the gauze bandages and presses. Theena readies another salve and the stitching supplies.

"Stop the blood, Geoff," Theena begs.

"I'm trying," he grumbles.

"Lift the gauze," Ránulf says.

"It couldn't have stopped bleeding, yet," Theena says, cautiously.

"Lift it," he repeats.

Theena lifts the gauze, which appears to have soaked through with Geoff's blood. The wound, however, is no longer bleeding. Ránulf cleans the wound and sutures it. He then places a gauze pad over it and tapes it securely. He walks to the back room of the kitchen and retrieves a small jar from a second refrigerator there. He pours liquid from the jar into a shot glass and brings it to Theena.

"Have Geoff drink this," he advises. She takes the glass and begins speaking softly to Geoff as Ránulf moves to the other side of the room where Amy and Dave are watching an unconscious Rowan like hawks.

Ránulf kneels beside Rowan and holds a small sachet under his nose. He gives it a slight squeeze and a small puff of dust shoots out. Rowan inhales it and begins to wake.

Chapter 36

Amy and Dave are in the living room, Amy feigning sleep on the couch. Dave is reading and absent-mindedly playing with the pentagram pendant on the necklace Ránulf gave him. Rowan, Theena, Geoff, and Ránulf all come into the room. Amy sits up. Rowan is back to normal, any spirit within him having been banished.

"So," Ránulf begins, "Rowan and Theena are going to start clean-up here at the house. Dave, if ye can help with the kitchen defrosting, it will go all the faster. Geoff, if ye can take the snowmobile back to the village. I don't want it sitting out all night, exposed, and also leaving the village without enough transportation in the snow. Amy will follow in the manor's snowmobile and give ye a ride back. I am going to study this book in hopes of reversing Allander's curse. And everyone, give up on the kitchen if it's not done by ten. Ye all need a bit o' rest."

"It's about five," Rowan says. "I can see what I can salvage in the kitchen for dinner."

"It's been a long day." Theena sighs half-heartedly.

"Amy and I will eat at the village, Rowan," Geoff says.

Ránulf walks upstairs with his book. The other five go into the kitchen to survey the work to be done.

"Look at this Christing mess," Dave mutters.

"We'll never unthaw all of this today," Theena states, flatly.

"The snowman froze this?" Geoff asks. "It's not as bad as what he did to the bookstore." Rowan's face saddens as he remembers his mother. "Shit, Rowan. I'm sorry."

"It's okay," Rowan says.

"The funeral is set for tomorrow at midnight," Geoff says. "That's what the villagers decided on."

Amy and Geoff leave for the village on the snowmobiles. Theena attempts to crack the ice around the refrigerator. Dave assists her while Rowan stares around the room, dumbly.

"How is it possible for him to create as much ice as this?" he wonders aloud. "Ránulf can't even throw a spell like this!"

"Those silver disks you talked about, could they help?" Dave asks.

"No," Rowan says."They only had a minimal effect on that snowball, anyway. They wouldn't be able to do anything for this."

"They're more powerful if Ránulf uses them," Theena says.

Rowan stands before the sink. He begins to chant and gesture like when he melted the ice statue of Ránulf. His hands harness a slight red aura, but the aura fades and nothing else happens.

"Shit!" Rowan curses.

"That's okay," Theena says soothingly. coming over to him. "You probably would have just melted the whole sink, anyway."

Rowan gives Theena one of Ránulf's dirty looks.

"Ránulf can fix this," he says. "You just wait." He leaves the room.

"Splendid," Theena mutters.

"He just didn't want to help thaw out the kitchen," Dave jokes to try and lighten the mood.

Meanwhile, Amy is following Geoff in the snowmobile. They slow down as they reach the outskirts of the village. Amy feels a strong occurrence of *deja vu*. The buildings were obviously made without the use of modern machines and contraptions but they looked exquisitely crafted. The village was smaller than Amy thought it would be. She pictured a bustling community of pagans dancing forever around a boiling cauldron but she only saw a small group leaving the village on foot and a woman entering a large, round building.

She follows Geoff to the snowmobile shed which was functioning like a small garage. It contained another snowmobile, a work bench, and loads of common household and field tools. As she dismounts from the snowmobile, she sees the stables that were attached to the back of the garage shed. Without even looking at Geoff, Amy hastens into the stables. Immediately the smell hit her. Not a bad smell, but a good, clean smell of fresh straw. Oh, how she suddenly fell in love with every animal in there. The sheep, the goats, the horses, and the cows! She was overjoyed, and *didn't* know why. She squealed like the newborn piglets in the corner stall on her left when Geoff laid his hand on her shoulder.

"Don't DO THAT!" she says, hysterically.

"Sorry," he says. "You just looked like you were studying

those goats too hard." They leave the stables and begin to walk around the village. The village was built around the large, round building. The homes surrounded it in a faithful pattern except a clearing for a small park. Children were playing on a wood playset connected to a large climbing block by a bridge made of rope and lumber.

Amy and Geoff reach the other side of the village which gradually gives way to a hill.

"Look," Geoff whispers, pointing as Amy gasps.

Atop the rise in the distance, a single black buck stood with his antlers rising proudly above his head.

"Ránulf's familiar?" Amy quietly asks.

"Yeah," Geoff says in an equal tone of voice.

They walk back to the shed and get on the snowmobile Amy brought down from the manor.

Amy's face contorts in a curious expression as she eyes a single black raven flitting from one bare tree to the top of another, cawing madly.

"Geoff—" she asks.

"It's an ill omen," he says. "It's one of Rowan's flock, but if one is alone, acting like that, it definitely means bad luck."

"Just great," Amy mutters. "I don't think we needed a portent for that." They leave the village.

Chapter 37

Ránulf is sitting in his room, reading. He doesn't hear the knocking at the door.

"Ránulf!" comes the voice of Rowan.

Ránulf doesn't acknowledge Rowan. He is studying the book with full attention. Finally, he looks up.

"Come in, Rowan," he says.

The door knob rattles.

"The door's locked," Rowan cries in mock despair.

Ránulf motions with his hand and the door opens.

"I hate when you do that," Rowan complains. "You know no one else can do that."

"Well," Ránulf says, closing his book, "I've been thinking of hooking up a *Clapper* to something or other so that it would take less energy. I'll leave that to Geoff who is more clever than I with gadgets."

Rowan's face turns serious.

"There's a discarnate presence here," he whispers. "I can't get a *fix* on it… or an alignment."

"Calm thyself," Ránulf says. "Please make the acquaintance of my variation of an *unseen helper* spell. It took six lunar months to cast, and now I can summon it at will for small tasks. Now, what is it tha's on about?"

"The ice in the kitchen—" Rowan says.

"Ye want me to make it disappear?" Ránulf asks.

"Well, yes," Rowan says. "I know you can. You're always doing little things like this unseen servant, balls of fire, and those little blue darts of light."

"It all depends," Ránulf says. "I've come up with a theory on how Allander created the ice. Almost the same theory on how I created that illusion of me trapped in the ice."

"That ice is no illusion," Rowan says. "It's cold and it's physically there. Dave and Theena are trying to break through it now. They've freed the refrigerator but I couldn't free the sink with that heat spell I learned from your notes."

"I'll come down so I can explain it to ye and the other two."

Ránulf rises. "*Lights out to please the night.*"

A gust of wind extinguishes the candles.

"Your invisible friend?" Rowan asks. Ránulf nods. They go downstairs and into the still mostly-frozen kitchen. Theena and Dave are fiercely trying to free the door to the wood burning stove.

"Stop putting yerselves out," Ránulf announces.

Theena and Dave stop and look at him questionably.

"Has this ice melted at all?" Ránulf asks.

"No," Theena says, sighing.

"Have ye gotten thyselves wet trying to clean this up?"

"No," Dave says, skeptically.

'That's because it's not real," Ránulf says.

"Bullshit," Dave responds. "Don't tell me this shit isn't *real*!"

"What is it then, Ránulf?" Theena asks.

"It's a trick o' the senses, that's all," Ránulf answers. "Real enough 'til ye know better."

"Then couldn't disbelief dispel it, if it's an illusion?" Rowan asks.

"Or if we willed it not to be here," Theena asks.

"No," Ránulf says with a sigh. "It's real to all five normal senses and only thy sixth sense can dispel it. Thy mind doesn't think it is ice, thy mind *knows* it is ice so ye have to *unknow* it. That's how convincing this sort of illusion is. Thy mind knows heat melts ice, so any heat ye apply dispels it. There would be no water... maybe just a slight vapor because this illusion wasn't cast for water, but for ice. Allander as the snowman is projecting his reality onto us and probably doesn't realize himself that it is a form of illusion."

"So are we helpless against it?" Rowan asks.

"Yeah," Dave adds. "Say the snowman shoots us with an ice blast—will it hurt us?"

"If thine own head tells ye it'll freeze, then it will," Ránulf says. "Ye have to convince thy mind and body that the ice is not there." He faces the center of the kitchen and stretches out his arms.

"Be silent a moment." Ránulf clears his mind. He goes over to the oven which is still iced. His hand passes through the ice and grasps the handle of the oven door. He opens the door to the oven as if the ice wasn't there. Then, the rest of the ice in the room is simply no longer there.

"How?" Dave asks in wonder.

"Ye watched my hand pass through the ice as if it wasn't there. Then, I opened the door. This impossibility convinced ye that the ice wasn't there."

"How come we can't do that?" Rowan asks. "I mean, make ourselves unaware of it?"

"It takes a still mind and total unawareness of the ice," Ránulf says. "I made myself forget the ice was there and that I had to open the oven."

"Will it still be here for Amy and Geoff?" Theena asks.

"No." Ránulf shrugs. "Our victory over the illusion has dispelled the energy that was maintaining it. The ice over at the shop was another story."

"It's still there?" Dave asks.

"No one's been there to be unaware of the ice," Ránulf explains. "Geoff wouldn't have known this."

"Can you do that to the snowman?" Dave asks.

"Aye," Ránulf says. "But then only I would be protected from it. And not from the ax, mind ye. It is still an entity swinging that weapon around."

"So," Theena summarizes, "in other words—no."

"No, because the snowman is made of real snow, now that I reckon it," Ránulf says. "Anyhow, let's get something cooking, I'm starving."

Chapter 38

It's getting dark. Amy and Geoff are speeding along in the snowmobile. Geoff is driving and Amy's arms are around his waist. They are quickly approaching the crest of a small hill. As they reach the top they are shocked to see that the other side of the hill is without snow *or* ice. The snowmobile stalls on the withered grass.

"Oh shit!" Amy gets off the snowmobile.

"What's wrong?" Geoff asks.

She points at the snowless ground.

"This isn't natural," she declares. "The snowman must have done it."

Geoff gets off the snowmobile and pushes it around the hill into the snow. He starts it back up.

"If that's what you think, then we'd better get back," Geoff says. Amy gets back on the snowmobile behind Geoff. Just as the lights of the house come in view, Geoff gasps. The snow in their path spreads away leaving a patch of barren ground. The snowmobile lurches onto the ground and stalls again.

"Let's just run to the house!" Amy cries, tugging on Geoff's arm.

"No," he says, quietly. "Just walk normally." They begin to walk up the barren path. The wind picks up just enough to make them both think that something terrible is on the verge of happening. Amy clings to Geoff.

"Visualize white light surrounding us," Geoff says, calmly. "It will protect us."

Amy stops, suddenly. As if in a fairy-tale she commands with great passion, "Kiss me, Geoff." She takes his kiss and presses into him. She quickly opens his coat and unbuttons his shirt.

"Amy," he whispers. "Don't... it's cold." She places her hands on his chest.

"I don't care," she says, practically panting. "I want you." She tries to put her hand down his pants, but he stops her by grabbing her wrist.

"Don't you have something going with Dave?" he asks.

"Dave is nothing," she says, shocked. " I only want you!"

She tries to touch his cock through his jeans and he backs away.

"No, Amy," he says.

"What are you?" she screams, hysterically. "A fag or something?"

"Amy," he says, "calm down. I just don't have any feelings for you."

"You bastard!" she screams. "I! Loved! You!" She pulls an ax out of nowhere.

"Amy, *don't*!" Geoff screams.

Her eyes glow red as she swings at him. He tries to grab the ax and gets the back of his wrist cut. He jumps back and she just barely misses with her next swing. She swings again, but he is able to kick the ax from her hand. Amy screams.

"Take it easy," Geoff begs, sounding out of breath.

Suddenly a scarf wraps around Geoff's neck from behind, the snowman holding it, having appeared soundlessly. It begins to choke Geoff.

Amy screams again and runs for the house.

Inside the house, Rowan is serving Theena, Dave, and Ránulf a dinner of baked chicken. Abruptly, Ránulf starts to choke. He drops his chicken and stands up, knocking over his chair.

"Geoff and Amy," he whispers. He takes his staff and runs for the back door. Rowan, Dave, and Theena follow.

Through the back door, they can see Amy running up to the house.

"Help!" she screams. "It's killing Geoff!" Rowan, Theena, and Dave rush off towards Geoff. Ránulf puts his arm around Amy, leads her into the kitchen, and they sit.

"Why don't you go?" she asks.

"Too late," Ránulf says, barely breathing. "The damage has been done. There is nothing I can do."

Rowan arrives at the scene first, Theena second, and Dave last. Rowan yells in grief and horror. Theena lets out a half-scream and Dave just stares, unable to process what he is seeing.

"It's too late," Theena whispers. Blood leaks from Geoff's mouth. The multi-colored scarf is still around his neck. Theena begins to cry.

"Dave," Rowan says, "help me…" He raises Geoff by his shoulders and Dave takes his legs. They get him onto the snowmobile and return to the house.

"We'll share the sad news at Rowena's funeral tonight," Ránulf says after they have all returned to the kitchen.

At 11:30 PM Ránulf, Rowan, Theena, Dave, and Amy get into the Suburban.

"We'll take the paved way to the village," Ránulf announces. They leave by way of Ránulf's driveway and arrive onto the state highway. They circle around the estate. At 11:46 they pull into a half-hidden, paved road. The road goes through the forest lit by lanterns every 25 feet along alternating sides. Most magnificent are the carved figures holding the lanterns. So elvish… Faerie-like… their wooden eyes seemed to invite you to come and stand vigil with them, eternally still.

"There's a car following us," Amy notices.

"Aye," Ránulf says. "Many will come to pay Rowena their respects and celebrate her life."

"And many will come to do the same for Geoff," Theena says, quietly.

The Suburban pulls out of the forest into a type of parking lot. There are no boundaries or cement, just some earth cleared of snow.

"This is where we get out and walk to the village," Rowan says. They walk for about a half mile and enter the village. The funeral is taking place in the big, open space in the center of the village. It has begun.

Two black-robed figures stand over the coffin. One male, the other female. A single long long note is sounded on a horn. Dave can see Bast lying beside the coffin. Three more black-robed figures stand near the outside of the circle.

"The horn is sounded for Rowena," one of them says loudly.

"So be it," comes a unified voice from people who've attended a funeral rite before. The female robed figure removes her hood.

"That tonight Rowena is not with us," she says, "here in the circle, saddens us all. Yet, let us try not to feel sad. For is this not a sign that she has fulfilled this life's work? Now she is free to move on. We shall meet again, never fear. And that will be a time for further celebration."

The priest removes his hood. "Let us send forth our good wishes to bear her across the Bridge," he says. "May she return at any time that she may wish, to be with us here."

Ránulf approaches the circle's border in his black robe. He makes some motions with his double-edged knife to make a door into the circle. He enters and seals the invisible portal behind him.

He stands at the altar behind the coffin.

"Let us all imagine Rowena as we best remember her," he says. The priest, priestess, and over half of the people congregated suddenly produce athames and point them at the coffin.

"Let us send Rowena love, joy, and happiness." Ránulf stands aside and signals for a period of silence. The silence lasts for about a minute. Amy shifts uneasily. The congregated witches are sending love and peacefulness to Rowena as she awaits in death for reincarnation. The priestess puts away her athame. Everyone else puts theirs away, as well, as the priestess stands to face the coffin.

"We wish you all the love and happiness we may," she intones. "We will *never* forget you. Do not you forget us.

Whenever we meet here, you are always welcome."

"So mote it be," come the unified voices again. The priest and priestess walk along the circle counter-clockwise, thus dispersing it. The coffin is carried to the large, round building and the funeral-goers follow.

"I've never been to a funeral like this before," Amy says to Dave. Dave smiles.

"I like it," he says. "It's enchanting."

The funeral lasts until 2:00 AM in the round building. Several people visit Rowena's corpse until it is removed at 1:30 in the morning. There is partaking of refreshments, light chatter, and meditation. Some folks leave and others just get comfortable on the earthen floor, there for the night.

At 2 AM, Ránulf drives Amy and Dave back to the house.

"I've news for ye," Ránulf says to them.

"Good or bad?" Dave asks, yawning.

"Good for us, bad for the snowman," Ránulf says, a touch of anger finally entering his voice.

"You figured out how to kill it?" Amy asks, wearily.

"No," Ránulf admits. "But the gods are on our side. It's supposed to warm up tomorrow and stay warm for about four days. That may be enough time for me to figure out what to do about the snowman."

"Thank God," Amy says with a sigh.

"Just be aware of what god ye are thanking, Amy," Ránulf advises.

"I don't mean to offend you," Amy says, "but I'm a Catholic and I only believe in one God."

"Do ye believe in Satan?" he asks her.

"Yes," she says. "I believe in the Devil."

"Do ye believe in the saints?" Ránulf asks. "Like Saint Patrick, Saint John, Saint Francis and such?"

"Yes," Amy answers, confused.

"What are Satan and Saint Peter if they be not gods?" Ránulf asks. "They have godly attributes and ye worship them, place them on your altars, carry their tokens."

"They're different," Amy asserts.

"There are saints of travel, saints of luck, saints of finding lost items, and those who are protectors of children," Ránulf continues. "They are just updated versions of gods of travel, goddesses of love, gods of luck, and other gods. And Satan is just the god of evil. He's based on a perversion of the old gods of the afterlife and underworld, such as the Greek god, Hades, and Egyptian god, Set."

"Satan isn't a god!" Amy begs. "That's ludicrous. He's the Devil!"

"Satan doesn't exist," Dave volunteers, wide-awake now. "Christian scholars created Satan from the gods of the Celts and the pagans."

"Correct, Dave." Ránulf takes a puff on his pipe as they begin up the main driveway. "They created Satan so they could criminalize the witches and pagans for worshipping him. Otherwise, how could they burn or hang those who weren't Christian? The ancient Romans, for example, wanted complete control of the masses that they had 'conquered'. They forced them into Christianity. The Roman officials were awed by witchcraft and tried to use it to their own ends. They twisted it, developing their own black magic and devil worship. Folk magic was a way of life for the majority of Western Europe. Many witches came to the New World after what is now New England was colonized by the British to escape religious persecution. Never mind that it ended up being just another monotheistic ruling class on this side of the pond."

"Never mind!" yells Amy, exasperated by the lecture. "I'm sorry I got you started. Not all of us are so attracted to false idols."

"Young lady!" Ránulf interrupts loudly as they pull to a stop in front of the house. "Thy 'god' is an angry, bearded old man who sits on a throne above the clouds all day doing nothing as his priests preach how evil this world is!"

"Jesus Christ died because of this evil world!" Amy counters.

"Jesus Christ is a bleeding, dead god on a cross," Ránulf snaps. "It makes me wonder what kind of people would worship an image as that. It's an executioner's construct. It's as if Christians are walking around wearing electric chairs hanging from their necks."

He cuts the engine. She throws open the door of the Suburban.

"Speaking of 'angry, bearded old men' who sit around doing nothing." Amy's voice is like acid. "You can't even keep the closest people around you alive!" She gets out of the vehicle and slams the door closed. Then, she shatters the night with a scream.

Ránulf and Dave get out of the vehicle and look up at the manor, stupefied. The entire house is covered in a transparent coat of ice. Dave walks up to it and touches it.

"Make it go away, Ránulf." He can barely get the words out. "Make it go away!" Tears spring from his eyes.

Ránulf walks to the house.

"I can't," he says, in a tone of disbelief. "This is real ice."

"Holy shit," Amy says.

They walk around the house to a cellar door that is free from ice.

"We'll go in here," Ránulf says as he unlocks it. They descend, Ránulf going last. Dave locates and activates a light switch.

The floor of the cellar is earthen and the walls are all black. A stone altar sits in the center of a large circle. The room is about 900 square feet, equal on all sides, with the only other door being on the opposite wall.

"What's this?" Amy asks.

"It's a circle!" Dave exclaims, beaming. "For rituals and stuff."

They shut off the light and go through the other door. The next part of the cellar is divided into two parts. One part would obviously be the washroom. The other resembled more of a living quarters, with a fireplace and a spiral staircase.

They ascend the spiral staircase into a room just slightly wider than the stairwell itself. The stairs continue up but they stop at the ground level and pass through a door into the main foyer of the house. Dave attempts to open the door to the exterior but the ice on the outside holds it fast.

"I shall take leave of ye now, to prepare for tomorrow as best I can," Ránulf says.

"I'm going to bed, Dave." Amy turns to go, her expression deadpan from exhaustion. "I'm hoping to sleep in tomorrow. It's been another long, horrible day and night."

"'Night," Dave says, hoping everyone's interactions are

improved in the morning. Then, he too, heads upstairs to retire for what's left of the night.

Chapter 39

Ránulf sits alone in his room with two white candles burning steadily. He only takes breaks from reading to write down notes. The book he is studying is entitled *The Daemon Witche*. No author is noted on its spine and he knows this is because the author was hung for witchcraft and the book went underground. Such a book would usually be a waste of Ránulf's reading time. Sixty years ago he would have read something like this. But even Ránulf at fifteen was too young to uncover the hidden meanings of a Crowley-like book such as this. This book was a complete affront to all magic-users, ecospiritualists, and supernaturalists. Ránulf had deduced it was written by a demented Catholic priest. A bishop, with close ties to the papacy. Ránulf didn't care who the pope was in 1391, or even the antipope. He didn't care if this book was written in Avignon, Rome, or even Constantinople.

Oh, the problems the papacy had, Ránulf thought. Now, they call worldwide meetings of bishops to try and put pieces of the Church back together, to staunch the outpouring of departing members. Homosexual priests who molest young boys seemed to be the forbidden topic of the day. Dave would think that was a cool name for a rock group.

Now, ladies and gentlemen, dudes and skirts! The band you've all been waiting for: Homosexual Priests Who Molest Young Boys! Then a thrash-punk band would appear on stage performing ridiculous lyrics.

"Oh heavy metal kill yourself. Pray to your mother, rape your Satan. Fuck your dog. Molest young boys. Light the candles, drip wax on your dick! Holy water makes good lubricant! Take a gun to your head—Suicidal! Satanistic! Bisexual! Cut my hair, I'll fuck your ass! I'm a priest and GOD's my lover!"

The satire would be utterly lost on Tipper Gore.

Ránulf extinguishes his candles. *If I stay up any later, I won't have enough strength to fight off half a snowman.*

Amy lies awake on her bed, reliving the events of the day over and over in her mind. *Why does something seem missing about the snowman killing Geoff? Something is blacked out. I don't know what. Did it possess me like it did Rowan? No, I'd know that. Wouldn't I?* She falls asleep.

Chapter 40

Early morning, at 6:13 AM, a blue car is driving away from the village. The candles in the lanterns are all burnt out along the road. The trees tower over the car almost frighteningly. A woman is driving, her baby girl asleep in her car seat in the back. She slows her car. A snowman is situated in the middle of the road.

Chapter 41

Ránulf is awoken by a raven tapping on his window. He sits up.

"Where?" he asks. He closes his eyes and quickly scries the location of the snowman.

A knock at Ránulf's door.

"Come in, Dave," he says. Dave enters.

"I won't ask how you knew it was me," Dave says. "I had a dream."

"Tell me on the way." Ránulf quickly sheds his soft, cotton pajamas onto the floor giving Dave an incidental view of his physique. Momentarily blushing, Dave takes in Ránulf's surprisingly toned musculature and the light, silver hair of his chest, abdomen, and bush.

Christ, Dave thinks, *Ránulf is hot… and hung!* Dave's dick twitches in the confines of his pants and he quickly looks away. "On the way…" he echoes and starts toward the door as Ránulf finishes dressing.

They run out the back door and get into the Suburban. As they're driving down the driveway, realization strikes Dave.

"The ice on the house is gone," he says.

"Aye, I noticed," Ránulf says. "I don't have time to guess at things right now, though. Tell me about thy dream."

"I can't remember it all," Dave admits. "Just something about a baby… and the hat. Shit! I hate it when I forget my dreams so fast!"

"A baby and a hat?" Ránulf asks.

The blue car is halfway off the road in a snowy ditch. The windshield is shattered and the woman is sprawled halfway out of the open car door. The car seat lacks the baby that had been there moments before. There are tracks of snow in the back seat and a baby's bib. The bib reads *Baby Angelique.*

"Angie…" the woman whispers and passes from our world. The coal eyes of the snowman stare into her forevermore in her own make-shift Hell.

Ránulf's Suburban arrives at the scene of the attack.

"Oh my god," Dave whispers.

Ránulf gets out of the vehicle, approaches the woman, and ascertains her condition.

"Blast it," he says through clenched teeth. "We're too late, sure as snow." He turns back toward Dave who is getting out of the vehicle to join him. Dave's eyes suddenly widen as a look of panic crosses his face. A scream approaches his lips but never makes it out.

The deceased woman rises behind and above Ránulf. He turns around.

"Oh!" he yelps, surprised, and falls backwards into the snow.

"Ránulf!" the spectral zombie wails. "He's taken Angelique! Oh, he's taken my Angie! And now you must stop the imp, oh the evil, evil child!" The corpse continues her pronouncement in a falsetto howl. "Your eyes will be deceived to see what he wants it to be! That child is no longer mine. Allander is in control of her mind!"

The scene is then completely normal. The woman is sprawled out of the open car door like before. Ránulf stands up. He brushes the snow and gravel from his rear as Dave locks his door, swiftly back in the Suburban. Ránulf gets in the vehicle and picks up a CB radio handpiece.

"Athame to Chalice," he speaks into the CB in code. "Over."

A male voice responds, "Yes, go ahead Ránulf."

"Let's stick to the codes, Chalice," Ránulf instructs him and adds, "Over."

"Sorry," Chalice apologizes. "Over."

"We have a code 4 on the road going out of the village,"

Ránulf says. "Please handle discreetly. Over."

"Christ in the toilet!" Chalice exclaims. "Code 4? I'll be right there. Chalice out."

In the midst of the snowy forest at 7:38 AM the rays of the sun are starting to shine through the branches. A baby's giggle can be heard. Little baby Angelique is putting on the snowman's hat.

At 7:45 AM the road is cleared. The blue car has been prepared for removal. The woman has been transferred to a sister coven for funereal arrangements. The police aren't too easily kept out. At 7:50 AM they appear at the manor.

The poor woman had no family besides baby Angelique. The witches were putting things in motion for her funeral as fast as was reasonable under the circumstances but the cops were racing against time, too. These two, in particular, were convinced the witches conducted human sacrifice out here on the estate. In fact, they would put money down that they had something to do with the rash of gruesome ax murders in the city. Oh, not *all* of the cops were convinced of that. Some cops were witches. More than that didn't care and not only a few Omaha cops were covertly Satanic. A couple of them on the force, true Satanism, and some misled Christian devil worshippers in the county Sheriff's office. The Satanists didn't perform sacrifices, but they didn't like being confused with the paganism that the witches practiced, giving them a bad name, in their opinion. Their perception, rather erroneous, being that the pagans weren't at peace until they'd gained the approval and acceptance of their gods or goddesses. That belief, they could not abide because they *knew* that there were no gods and even if there were, they certainly didn't care about us. "Believing anything other than that we all contain our own divinity is naivete in its most embarrassing form," they might inform you, scornfully.

Ránulf answered the door for these two fine policemen. They are both white Christians, but of different denominations, such an insignificant differentiation in his mind. The one who rang the doorbell, Steve Pellon, was a good little Catholic boy; except for the fact that he's 48 and beats his wife. The other, a 29-year-old Italian-American named Tony Michaels, was a Methodist, having converted against his family's wishes when he married. He hadn't been to church since he was seventeen. That was when he stole a crucifix as a dare. He stole many things as a teen but he was rarely caught. He got caught stealing that crucifix, though. The pastor decided not to press charges if Tony enrolled in a police academy. The rest was history.

Ránulf invited Tony and Steve in for hot herbal tea. Tony accepted, but Steve was caught up in his own fantasies of poison and murder. Amy served them.

"Just let us see the body, Wylkyn," Steve says.

"She died in a car wreck and the accident was reported," Ránulf says. "What else do ye want?"

"She had a little girl," Tony says.

"Angelique is at the village," Ránulf responded.

"We're going to get an order for an autopsy from the court," Steve says.

"We do things our own way here, Steven," Ránulf chides him in dismissal. "Good day, deputies." He shows them to the door.

"We'll be back, *wizard*," Steve says. "Count on it."

Ránulf locks the door behind them. Steve and Tony get in their car and depart down the drive.

"Why don't you like these people, Steve?" Tony asks.

"They're Devil worshippers," Steve says, acidly. "Every God-forsaken one of them. And I'm going to bring them down. That woman was sacrificed and the courts won't order an autopsy, let alone issue a warrant."

"Hasn't a search warrant been ordered before on this place?"

"Oh, yes." Steve smiles. "When it first was set up. Right before I joined the force. The chief thought they were having black masses and sacrifices so he talked the judge into awarding a warrant. They went in and found an altar and shit in the basement and the floor had a big pentagram circle on it. They also found a lab of some kind, with all kinds of herbs and potions."

"So what happened?" Tony asked.

"Ránulf Wylkyn was arrested and thrown in jail. Hot fire and fuck, what I wouldn't have given to see that old bastard in jail! Then later, before the judge, he claimed freedom of religion about some shit called Wicca or something. Which, to me, is just a fancy name for witchcraft and Satanism. So Wylkyn was freed. The chief and the judge who pursued and issued the warrant both lost their jobs. The weirdest thing is that no one could get Wylkyn's real name. He was already known in Europe for his voodoo-witchcraft, and after that he was known in Nebraska. It seems he came to Omaha to get away from 'religious prejudice'. He had previous records in California and South Dakota. I guess he had a whole mountain estate where all the witches and bitches ran around naked fucking demons and shit."

"He doesn't seem like he would be like that," Tony commented.

"Well, he is like that," Steve says.

They begin to drive up the road to the village.

"Where are we going?" Tony asks, igniting a cigarette with the car's lighter.

"To the witch-village, just to look around," Steve replies.

"We can get canned for coming up here!" Tony exclaims with worry.

"No..." Steve laughs. "I tore off the *No Trespassing* sign two years ago. They haven't put up a new one, yet."

On the side of the road, something catches Tony's eye.

"Stop, Steve," Tony says. He places his hand on Steve's arm.

"What?" Steve asks. "You want me to suck you off?" He stops the car.

"No, I thought I saw someone running through the trees," Tony says. He gets out of the car.

"Probably some damn witch," Steve grumbles.

"No," Tony says."It was a little girl, I think."

They both see it this time.

"There." Tony points as she disappears into the trees.

"I'll go around this way, Tony," Steve says and runs off into the woods. Tony walks off the road, through a drift, and into the forest. He sees small shoe-prints in the snow and begins to follow them. After a few minutes, the footprints stop at the base of a tree. Tony looks up to see a small girl in the tree eating a rabbit, raw. There is blood on her face and running down the trunk. She must be at least 3-4 years old.

Tony gasps.

"You know," the girl says to no one in particular, "I've never eaten a rabbit before. I haven't even eaten anything in 13 years."

This is absurd, Tony thinks, trying to calm himself. "You're not even close to 13 yet. What's your name?"

"Why," she begins, feigning offense, "I'm Angelique and I'm 108. I was 95 when I died. You'll be 29."

Tony is speechless. Angelique snaps the rabbit in half.

"Want a bite?" she asks, blood dripping from her mouth.

"No," Tony pants in sickness.

"Oh please!" she begs. "I can't eat it all by myself and I didn't kill it for nothing!"

"No," he says. "I'll be leaving now."

"No!" she screams in the siren-like voice of a banshee. "I want you now!" Her voice suddenly changes to a growl. "My virgin sex is crying for you!" She begins to cackle, hysterically.

Tony flees the grotesque horror as the trees begin to bleed into the snow. He can hold it in no longer, he screams.

"Steeeeeeve!"

It is the last thing Tony Michaels ever says. Angelique hunts him down and begins to eat him like the tasty hare she just devoured.

Steve is sitting in the cruiser. His pants and underwear are around his ankles. His right hand is pumping his tool as his left one cradles his hairy scrotum. He groans, close to ejaculation.

He stops stroking. Did he hear his name being called? He quickly stops his fantasy and dons his pants. He steps out of the car.

"Tony?" he hollers.

No answer.

He walks into the trees.

"Tony?" he cries, loudly.

Then he sees him.

Steve's latest meal hurls forth, cutting off his scream. He begins to choke on his vomit and reaches for a tree to steady himself. He spits bright red into the snow.

"Fucking Devil worshippers!" he cries.

Then he sees movement in the trees. He unholsters his gun. Theena's wolf, Timbre, bounds onto the scene.

Two gunshots echo through the still air of the estate at 8:40 AM. The first one hits the majestic wolf in the throat. The second, hits a tree.

The gunshots alert the witches in the village, who were just waking up from last night's funeral. For no apparent reason, Theena begins to cry, uncontrollably. Rowan puts a comforting arm around her.

"Theena?" he asks. "What's wrong?"

"I don't know." She pushes Rowan away gently and puts on her coat. She closes her eyes for a moment. "Timbre!" she cries. She runs from the building.

The telephone rings at the manor.

"You have a phone?" Amy asks as she opens her eyes from her nap on the couch.

Ránulf ignores her and picks up the receiver.

"Hello?" he says.

"Athame? This is Chalice."

"Matt!" Ránulf says impatiently. "Ye can use our real names on the telephone!"

"Sorry, Rán," Matt says. "Our police-friend, Steve, has called an ambulance from the road going into the village."

Ránulf closes his eyes and in his mind he sees Steve standing by his patrol car. He sees what is left of Tony, Timbre dead, and Theena and Rowan rushing to the scene. In half a mile, they will be there.

"Dummy up everyone," Ránulf says. "No one goes out of the village. When the police come to the village, lock up. *No one goes out.* Got that, Matthew?"

"Yeah, sure," Matt says. "Bye." He hangs up.

"What's wrong, now?" Amy asks.

"Dead cop," he says, stonily. "David!"

Dave comes out of the library into the living room.

"Come with me," Ránulf commands.

Chapter 42

Steve is inside his car again and doesn't see or hear Rowan and Theena approach. They run past him into the woods. When Theena sees the still, bloody form of Timbre, she screams.

"Oh, Goddess no!" Her tears stream down her face.

"Oh Timbre," Rowan gasps.

Theena cradles Timbre in her arms.

Rowan looks at Tony's devastated body.

"What in everwinter happened here?" he asks aloud. "What were the cops doing on the property?"

Presently, the sirens of an ambulance can be heard approaching; yet another unwelcome sound piercing the silence of the morning.

"Back away from the corpses," demands Steve's voice as he enters the scene, hand on his holster. Rowan pulls Theena away from Timbre.

"What happened here?" Rowan asks in a tone of authority.

"Who the hell are you that it's any of your business ?" Steve demands.

"I'm Rowan," Rowan replies, growing impatient, angry. "I'm the second-manager of the estate, right under Ránulf."

"Rowan?" asks Steve. "Give me your real name, not your devil-name."

Rowan's unkindness of ravens gather in the nearby trees. Steve casually points his gun at them and prepares to fire.

"You shoot that gun one more time on this estate," Rowan threatens, "and it will cost you your job, family, and your closest drinking buddies."

Steve lowers his weapon and opens his mouth as if to say something else stupid. Saved by the siren, the ambulance arrives and the EMT's rush out to meet him.

Ránulf and Dave arrive shortly. Two city police cars and the county coroner have joined Steve's cruiser and the ambulance at the scene. Tony was pronounced dead on arrival. Consequently, the deputies and paramedics want to take Timbre to check for abnormalities. A detective and a crime-scene investigator are making quick work of their review of Tony's circumstances while the coroner takes Polaroids. Matt is arguing with a white paramedic and a Black officer, both women. His appearance is clean-cut in his flannel overcoat, jeans, and boots.

"Neither of them had any business coming on the estate!" Matt argues.

"I'm not here to say whether that's true or not true," the officer says calmly, "but it's normal procedure for us to take the animal to the lab."

"I don't want my familiar ripped apart and tainted with your tools," Theena cries.

"We can arrange for you to receive the wolf back, ma'am," the paramedic informs her.

Ránulf walks up to the arguing group.

"Oh great," the officer says. "It's Ralph."

"That's Ránulf, dear lass," he says.

"And it's Tanya—Officer Tate," she corrects herself. "We have a small problem."

"There's no problem," Ránulf assures her. "Ye plainly see the wolf attacked the young officer?"

"Yeah, but—" Officer Tate stammers.

"No buts," Ránulf says. "The animal is a protected part of the estate under our nature preserve status and it will stay here."

Finally, the paramedics settle for blood and bone marrow samples from Timbre. Theena and Rowan wrap Timbre in a wool blanket and put her in Ránulf's Suburban. As the ambulance and deputies leave, a van containing a channel 6 news-team drives slowly up the road toward them.

"Matthew! Rowan!" Ránulf bellows. "Reporters!" Ránulf, Rowan, and Theena dash into the Suburban and drive off.

"Hey!" Dave yells.

"Dave, come on!" Matt yells. Dave gets in Matt's pickup truck and they start to head in the direction the news van is coming from. Suddenly, it pulls over and blocks the road. A pale woman heavily caked with make-up jumps out holding a microphone and dragging its cable after her as she walks to Matt's truck.

"We let RAY-noof get away, but we need to ask you a few questions," she says. She tosses back her hair, highlighted the night before with a box of Nice'n Easy Medium Blonde from the corner Rexall's.

Matt gets out of his truck and reluctantly walks to meet her, the unusually warmer breeze making a gentle sweep through his short, black hair.

"Go up to the house, Miss Jenners," Matt says. "I or Ránulf will speak to you there."

"Thanks Matt," she says and gets back into the van. Matt gets into his truck and proceeds to follow the van up to the house.

"I take it you know her?" Dave asks.

"Yeah," Matt says. "Whether we like it or not… mostly not… Steve's our cop and Sarah Jenners is our reporter."

"Are they both out to prove you're all a bunch of Satanists?" Dave asks.

"Steve is," Matt says. "But Miss Jenners is just hungry for any story we give her because we won't typically let her or the press onto the estate."

"So what happened back there, anyway?" Dave asks.

"From what I gather," Matt says, puzzling it together, "that 'good' policeman Steve and his partner trespassed onto our land in hopes of catching us witches doing something we're not supposed to be doing. But Tony wandered into the woods and Theena's familiar, Timbre, attacked and killed him."

"Theena's familiar?" Dave asks.

"Yes," Matt says, "but that doesn't seem right to me. None of the animals on the estate are vicious, especially not the familiars. She must have been on edge or overprotective with the recent deaths."

They pull into Ránulf's driveway and arrive at the house. Matt shows Miss Jenners and her cameraman into a study area, tidied up for guests without the usual herbs or signature decorative elements of the rest of the manor. The camera man unfortunately isn't allowed to bring his equipment in. Only a tape recorder. Ránulf and Rowan join them in the study. Amy and Theena are upstairs in Theena's room, Theena inconsolable over Timbre's death. Miss Jenners sits down.

"Tea?" Rowan offers.

"Yes, please," she says. Rowan excuses himself to the kitchen.

"So," Ránulf says, "I suppose ye want the story of the policeman who called wolf?"

"Your side of the story, Ray," she says.

"Sarah," Ránulf growls. "I've told ye innumerable times not to call me that."

"Yeah, I know," Sarah Jenners says, "But it's a million times easier to remember how to pronounce." She presses the "record" button on her tape recorder.

"This morning," Sarah starts, "the operators of the emergency CB channel in Douglas County, Nebraska, received an urgent summons for an ambulance and police back-up from deputy sheriff Steven Pellon. So far, as reported, a deputy was found dead, apparently mauled by a wolf. Ránulf, could you please tell me what the police were doing in your forest?"

"Steven Pellon and Anthony... Michaels, I dare say," Ránulf begins. "Anyway they came by inquiring about the tragic death of a young woman who drove her car off the road early this morning. She was Wiccan, so she was looked after our way. The officers wanted to get permission for an autopsy but I denied it, as her will instructed that she be looked after by the way of her coven. She will be cremated this afternoon, Goddess rest her soul."

"But," Sarah says,"this is the second such report of a death of one of your witches in 4 days. The death of Vicky Blackwood, known to witches as Rowena, was from a cause unknown. She was reported dead Christmas Eve by Geoff Etchins, representing your estate. Then, Gail Barker ran off the road and died this morning; her baby, Angelique, being taken care of at your village?"

"Aye," Ránulf says. "The legal papers will be signed by next week, I'd wager."

"It is reported that Deputy Sheriff Pellon and Deputy Michaels stopped up here this morning to question you. Then where did they go?" Sarah asks.

"Obviously," Ránulf says,"they drove up our private road to the village, illegally. Before they could get to our village, Deputy Michaels decided to romp in our forest where he was, sadly, mauled by a wolf."

"Do you have any idea why they would've tried to go to your village?" she asks. "When it is off-limits? Did they have probable cause or a search warrant?".

"No," Matt says. "Pellon has long been making himself an enemy to us. He still thinks we're evil or Satanic, even after *your* true, on-air reports of us!"

"He was seen removing the 'No Trespassing' sign on the road to the village a couple years back," Rowan volunteers.

"Well," Sarah says, sighing and shutting off the tape recorder. "I think that will be all I need for now." She finishes her tea. "I think I'll go get Pellon's side of the story."

Matt shows her and her camera-less cameraman to the door.

They leave and Matt returns to sit back down.

"Okay Ránulf," Rowan says, sternly. "There's no way that Timbre killed that cop."

"I know," Ránulf says. "Allander killed him, it's likely, and Timbre risked her life to save the village and covenstead. If no murderer would have been found, cops would have been crawling all over this place. They would have found out that Geoff is dead and that baby Angelique is missing."

"What happened to the baby?" Matt asks.

"The snowman got it, didn't it, Ránulf?" Dave says.

"I'm almost positive of it," Ránulf says. "But sooner or later, the cops will put things together."

"Such as?" Dave asks.

"That two of thy friends were horribly murdered," Ránulf starts off. "That Amy's entire family was murdered and ye are here with Amy, now. And that three of our witches have died, and one deputy. They will be asking a lot more… *unavoidable*… questions very soon."

Theena and Amy are still in Theena's room.

"I can't believe she's dead," Theena says, feeling the loss in her heart and soul. "I just can't!"

"Me either," Amy says. "She was an incredible animal. I've never seen a wolf like that."

"I guess she's better off where she is," Theena says, wiping the moisture from her eyes and face. "Awaiting reincarnation."

"You guys believe in reincarnation?" Amy asks impatiently.

"So did Christians until 553 C.E.," Theena explains.

"C.E.?"

"Common Era. It's what we say instead of A.D. because A.D. is a Christian term referring to a mythological event."

"There's no escaping Christianity is there?" Amy admits.

"Not completely," Theena says, regretfully.

"Then maybe it's true," Amy suggests, more gently.

"I don't think so." Theena laughs. "And I'm far from the only one who thinks that."

"Let's not talk about religion, Theena," Amy says, looking away.

"We should get ready for Geoff's funeral," Theena says.

"What time is the funeral?" Amy asks.

"It's at 1:00," Theena says. "That gives us about an hour and I think we all need to eat."

"I'll help," Amy offers, smiling. They go to the kitchen.

Chapter 43

Scene: An Omaha police cruiser is driving down the highway. Inside are Officer Tanya Tate and another police officer.

"I didn't know we had jurisdiction out here," he says.

"We normally wouldn't," Tanya starts to explain, "but with the population out at the estate growing, the county can't keep up with watching it. So, the state gave Omaha provisional jurisdiction over it."

"Interesting," he says. "Hey, pull down this dirt road."

"Why?" Tanya asks slyly. "Jason, what are you thinking?"

"You know what I'm thinking," Jason says. "The same thing I'm always thinking when I'm with you."

They pull off the highway and stop on the side of the dirt road, staying off the snowy edge. They both begin to strip.

"Oh baby!" Tanya yells, laughing. "Let's get a look at that meat!"

"I love how dirty you get when your clothes come off," Jason replies, smiling. He gets out of the car, buck naked.

"Baby!" Tanya yells. "Get your butt back in here. Don't be flappin' that thing in the wind!"

He opens up the back door and gets inside the back of the cruiser.

"Why don't you come back here with me, babe?" Jason taunts as he starts to pump his girthy penis to full stiffness. "I'm just getting warmed up."

"Go, Jason, get busy!" she chants. She blasts the heat and quickly runs out to join him in the back seat. She mounts him, guiding his shaft inside of her, and begins to *ride* him.

"Go, Jason, get busy," she chants again as she writhes atop him. "Go, Jason, get busy" nearly breathless this time. Jason grunts, wordlessly.

Suddenly all four doors fly open and then slam shut as the car's siren chokes out an impossibly brief broken wail.

Tanya yells out loud and covers her breasts with her hands. "What in the—"

Angelique's face appears over the front seat, behind the cage-like screen separating the two sections of the vehicle. She appears to have aged two more years since the morning.

"What are you guys doing?" Angelique asks, innocently.

"Nothin' baby," Tanya says. "Now go on home to your mama."

"But I want to watch!" Angelique begs. She presses the power lock switch for the back doors.

"Oh shit, Tanya," Jason says. "These doors won't open from the inside!"

"Little girl," Tanya asks, calmly. "Could you come open one of these back doors?"

"No," Angelique says. "I want you to finish what you were doing!"

"No, you little bitch!" Tanya yells. "Let us the fuck out of here!"

Angelique turns around and starts the car.

"Hey!" Jason screams. "Stop it!"

Angelique picks up the revolver from Jason's holster which still lies in the front seat.

"Hey kid," Tanya cries in a panic. "Don't be playin' with that. Put it down."

Angelique points the weapon at Tanya.

"You have a big mouth," Angelique says. "Bitch."

She pulls the trigger.

Jason screams as Tanya's blood covers his face, chest, genitals, and legs. Angelique begins to drive.

"Oh my God!" Jason continues to scream. "Stop! Let me out! I'll do anything…" His voice trails off. The little girl is gone. "Oh... fuck!"

The police cruiser speeds up to 120 MPH as it tears down the highway. It lurches to the east down another less-traveled road. Then, Jason sees the Missouri River in the distance.

"STOP!" he blurts. The animated car doesn't listen. It swiftly approaches the river. The river where Jason is later found drowned inside the cruiser at the bottom with his murdered lover.

Geoff Etchins' funeral was quite similar to Rowena's, except with only about half the attendees. After the ritual, Ránulf takes Amy aside.

"Amy?" he asks, quietly. "What do ye remember about Geoff's death?"

"The snowman choked him to death with its scarf, I think," she says.

"Do ye remember anything else?" Ránulf asks. "It's important."

Amy hesitates.

"I think I may have blacked out right before he died. I don't know!"

Ránulf drives Dave, Amy, Rowan, and Theena back to the house. That night, Amy retires early. Rowan attends to some duties at the village. Theena, Dave, and Ránulf sit in the library.

"I dare say it shall be us three who fight the snowman in the end," Ránulf worries. "Rowan has once been tainted by Allander's possession, and though no one saw Geoff die, it seems likely that Amy was possessed, too."

Bast walks out of nowhere into the library.

"So?" Theena asks. "What's the plan, Ránulf?"

"I can summon the snowman," Ránulf declares. "Figure I can contain him in a consecrated circle. But… I am not sure what to do from there."

"Destroy the hat," Theena says.

"What about that baby?" Dave asks.

"Angelique Barker," Ránulf replies.

Theena gasps. "Gods, yes. I completely forgot about Gail's baby!"

"The weather was a bit warmer today," Ránulf announces. "We all know Nebraska winters are quite unpredictable. The high for tomorrow is expected to be an impressive 54 degrees. Of course, all the snow won't melt but it should not be possible for the snowman to stay corporeal. It's likely Allander has already taken another form."

"The baby?" Dave asks in shock.

"Well, I know that *Timbre* didn't partially eat deputy Michaels," Ránulf says.

"Oh!" Theena gasps. "You're not saying the baby did it? That's sick!"

"I am indeed saying… the baby did it, possessed by Allander, of course. I also believe that Angelique's body is near."

"How near?" Dave asks. "And do you have to say 'body.'" He feigns a shiver.

"Quite near," he says. "I reckon we should search the house."

"I'll check on Amy," Theena volunteers, standing up.

Ránulf motions for her to wait.

"Take this." He hands her a silver disk with the symbol for air on it.

"Allander… or Angelique… is playing for keeps now, I'm sure. This will give you one burst of wind to save your life. It won't work inside very well so concentrate hard, then flee. I can't have another death on my hands."

Theena takes the disk and Bast follows her out of the library. Ránulf takes his staff and skirts behind a bookcase in the library where there are stairs going down.

"Where do these go?" Dave asks, following.

"My lab," Ránulf says. "Where I grow herbs and make healing infusions and various other potions. Theena often assists me as my botanical sciences apprentice."

They go through a door at the bottom of the stairs into a room smelling of earth and aromatic plants. Dave can recognize the scents of peppermint and roses but the other smells are new to him. Something flowery— *is that lavender?* he wonders.

"I think we should have started in the attic," Dave says, focusing.

"Logical," Ránulf admits, "but I need something from down here."

He opens the door into the washroom, and they continue past the lounge with the spiral staircase.

"So… Ránulf," Dave observes. "That's not exactly in the phone book."

Ránulf smiles faintly. "No, I suppose it isn't. It was my grandfather's name. Comes from the Old Country. It translates to *Raven Wolf* — a name meant to ward off death, in a sense. Up until recently, it's earned its keep."

They walk into the ritual space with the altar and circle. Ránulf walks up to the altar and depresses a hidden catch under its rim. A small compartment opens on the surface exposing a black-handled athame. Ránulf grasps it.

Theena is walking up the stairs which lead from the living room to the upstairs hallway. She goes left around a corner, opening the bathroom door and the door to Rowan's room. She opens the door to her room and the door to the stairs which lead to the third floor. She grasps the handle on Geoff's door and slowly turns it, peeking inside. She is surprised to realize that she hadn't noticed Matt had moved into the house from the village. Matt is standing in the room with his back toward her, naked. He is staring out the window at the moon. She clears her throat and Matt turns his head.

"Door's open," she informs him. "Look out for a little possessed baby." Theena opens the door all the way and leaves.

Matt dons a robe and returns to his meditation, bringing his gaze back to the moon.

Theena finds Ránulf's door locked. She opens Dave's door and as she starts to leave, her eyes catch a glimpse of his electric guitar. She goes into the room, considers a moment, and plugs in the amp.

Amy sits up in bed. A candle is lit and flickering behind the curtains of her bed. She throws them open. Bast is lying curled-up on the floor.

"Bast." Amy sighs as she goes to lift the cat. Bast hisses and Amy withdraws.

"What's wrong, kitty?" Amy asks.

"I think it's me," comes a small girl's voice from the other side of the bed.

Amy jumps back.

"Who's there?" she asks.

A small girl walks into view from behind the bed. She is finely garbed except for the odd-looking, sickeningly familiar stocking cap on her head.

"Who are you?" Amy asks, dreading her suspicion. "What are you doing in here?"

"I am Angelique," she pips. "I just thought I would come in here. I was following the kitty."

Amy turns to where Bast was, but Bast is gone. *Was she there before?* She tries to concentrate but is experiencing a frustrating case of brain fog.

"Bast?" Amy asks, urgently. Then she turns back to Angelique. "Well the kitty's gone, so maybe you should go, too."

"No," Angelique says, standing up. "I'll just watch you get ready like I used to watch my mother before she died."

Amy goes to the water basin in front of the mirror. Maybe splashing some water on her face will help wake her back up a little. She feels sorry for the girl.

"How did she die?" Amy asks as she lightly splashes her face. She reaches for a small towel and pats her face dry. As she looks into the mirror, where Angelique should be in the reflection, she is not. Instead, the vision of the snowman looms, large and impossible.

"The snowman killed her," Angelique answers.

Amy jumps away from the mirror, her back to it now, while watching Angelique. The snowman-in-the-mirror's stick-arms begin to reach out from inside the mirror.

"The hat!" Amy tries to collect her thoughts. "You have the hat?"

Angelique looks puzzled as she touches the hat.

"Please," Amy begs. "Give it to me!"

The water in the basin begins to freeze until it transforms into wet snow. The stick-arms begin to form the snow into a spherical shape.

"I can't give you this hat," Angelique says, shocked. "It was a very special gift to me."

Amy rushes Angelique and tries to take the hat. Tears begin to flow from Angelique's eyes.

"No!" Angelique cries. "It's not yours, it's mine!" Angelique grips the hat to her head, almost covering her eyes. Amy pushes her to the floor. Angelique screams. Suddenly, Bast pounces on her head, howling. Angelique screams again, blood running down her face. She grasps the cat and pulls her from her head, then hurls her through the closed, second-story window, shattering the glass.

"Bast!" Amy screams, horrified.

"Damn cat!" Angelique stands up and glares at Amy.

Amy runs for the door and screams when she can't open it.

"Help!" she cries. "Let me out!"

In Dave's room, Theena is playing a soft, slow ballad on Dave's guitar. She stops. Did she hear something? She unplugs the amp, places the guitar back on its stand, and leaves Dave's room. She opens the door to a guest room and slowly proceeds down the hall towards Amy's room. Snow is blowing into the hallway from under Amy's door.

Theena pulls out her magic, silver disk.

Ránulf and Dave are still in the basement. Ránulf has been showing him the uses of some of the sacred ritual tools. Suddenly, he places a chalice back down.

"David, go upstairs," he says, tone serious.

"Why?" Dave asks.

"Whenever ye question me in critical circumstances, it puts everyone at risk!" he snaps.

Dave turns heel and runs toward the stairs.

Ránulf begins to pour sea salt onto the earthen floor. Patterns begin to emerge in various designs as he pours. He concludes with an equilateral triangle pointing at a wide circle, which he then sits in the center of.

Meanwhile, Angelique has Amy cornered in her room. Amy takes her pentagram necklace and holds it out in front of Angelique.

"That can't help you, now," Angelique says, in her chipper voice, toying with her. "It was just so I couldn't find you magically."

Neon purple fire begins to crackle around Angelique's hands.

"Let's get this over with," she says. "I can feel Ránulf trying to call me."

The purple fires roar, fan out, and surround Amy.

Amy screams as the violet flames reach into her eyes, nose, mouth, and genitals… and pull her insides out.

The door to Amy's room bursts open as Theena barges in, wielding the silver disk. She sees a smoking figure collapse against the far wall as Angelique turns to her. It doesn't look right. There are guts, blood, and what smells like burnt shit all over.

Theena holds the disk facing Angelique and utters a short phrase as she visualizes Angelique blowing away. The disk glows white as a gale force wind begins to blow Angelique towards the broken window.

"No!" Angelique cries. She grabs onto the window ledge as she is lifted from the floor. Theena runs to the window and kicks her in the face, causing her to let go and be subsequently blown from the house. She turns to Amy… and recognizes her. She screams.

Matt gets there first and refuses to let Dave see the corpse. Ránulf arrives shortly, using the spiral staircase to his room, then walking down the hall to meet Theena outside of Amy's room. He enters the room with Theena. Matt and Dave wait in the hall. Dave is frantic. He was starting not to like Amy when she would get religious on them, but she was all he had to cling to of his old life, before the snowman.

Amy's body is covered by a sheet, saturated with her body's fluids. Ránulf lifts it and nearly chokes. He gazes at her, then places the sheet back in place.

"Amy is quite dead," Ránulf says. "I've never seen anything like this before. For now, we will have to keep her death secret."

Theena looks at Ránulf, she is crying.

"I was not expecting this, my dear," Ránulf says. He embraces her. "Theena, please ask Matt to go fetch Rowan. Tonight, I shall confront Allander... somehow. We have underestimated him at every juncture."

"It wasn't a baby," Theena says, breaking the embrace. "It was a small girl."

"Of course," Ránulf realizes."His possession of her has sped up her metabolism."

"I've never heard of a case of possession like that," Theena says.

"Well, Allander knew more than his fair share about the occult and supernatural before he died. Most entities or spirits don't have that… *occupational* advantage. Truly, though, I do not know what happened, or how, except that Allander was in here again despite my protection spells cast on the house and estate."

Ránulf and Theena leave the room to go downstairs with Dave. Matt begins the gruesome process of removing the body.

Ránulf, Dave, and Theena regroup in the library. Theena silently gives Ránulf the used silver disk, then she departs for the kitchen.

Dave is thumbing through a drawer in the library's small card catalog. He is looking up "Ghosts". Three books that catch his eye are *Ghost Spells,_Ghosts and Exorcisms,* and *Banishing Ghosts*. Dave locates *Ghost Spell*s and *Ghosts and Exorcisms* on their respective shelves. After considering a moment, he returns *Ghosts and Exorcisms* to its place and takes *Ghost Spells* with him and leaves the large room.

Rowan gets a message in the village to return to the house at once. He begins to run, checking to see that his sword is secure in its sheath. Immediately anxious of another snowman attack, he didn't know that Jacob Allander was now in control of Angelique Barker's body. Rowan also didn't know that Angelique was waiting for him on the way back to the house, hunting for her next victim. What he did know, with his senses on full alert, was that something evil was near and was a threat. Wisely, he visualized himself at the center of a globe of dark light, dimming his ability to be perceived by others. So, Angelique waited in hiding, but did not notice Rowan on his return to the house.

Rowan steps in the back door, and takes his boots off in front of the pantry. He goes through the kitchen and dining room and sees Dave reading *Ghost Spells* on the couch.

"Where's the old guy?" Rowan asks. "The message sounded urgent."

"He's either in his room," Dave flatly says, not looking up, "or downstairs in the circle."

Rowan decides to try downstairs. He goes to the door closest to the front door in the entryway. He descends the spiral stairway into the lounge. Sure enough, Ránulf is sitting in the middle of the circle. He stands up when Rowan enters.

"It's okay," Ránulf says. "The circle is not cast."

"What are you doing?" Rowan asks.

"Memorizing a ceremony which I hope will rid us of Jacob Allander and the snowman," he says.

"Why did you have me return to the house?" Rowan asks.

"Because we are all in too much danger to be running around while a possessed little girl is killing people," Ránulf answers. "Amy is no longer with us."

"No," Rowan whispers, shocked.

"Aye," Ránulf says, his brow furrowing. "I am afraid so. Please lock everything up. I'll cast a variation of a *watcher* spell so I shall be alerted if Angelique gets inside the house again."

Ránulf goes up the spiral stairs to his room. Rowan checks all of the windows and doors, including the new window in the living room the snowman had previously broken. He places plastic over Amy's broken window and locks her room up.

Except for Dave, no one's sleep is interrupted that night. Dave doesn't sleep at all. *Ghost Spells* isn't a very thick book but it contains a lot of information. It includes chapters on summoning ghosts, banishing ghosts, speaking with ghosts, punishing ghosts, binding ghosts, using ghosts to accomplish one's desired needs, and spectral divination.

Dave reads the chapter dealing with punishing ghosts. It tells how to karmically punish spirits from afar. Unfortunately, an item belonging to the deceased is needed. The snowman never left any souvenirs.

Finally, after pondering the idea for almost an hour, Dave decides to summon Amy's ghost. Dave puts on his jacket, takes another jacket from a chair in his room, and climbs the creaking stairs to the third floor. He steps out onto a balcony patio. He arranges some white candles around the small patio and sits down on one of the patio chairs. At the table where he is sitting, he lights one candle. He is holding Amy's coat and focusing on her image.

"Amy," he whispers.

A breeze flickers the candles as Dave continues to concentrate.

"Amy," he whispers again. "Can you hear me?"

"Dave?" comes an echoing female voice.

"Is that you, Amy?"

A pause.

"Yes," comes the haunting voice.

"We need your help," Dave says, holding tightly to his fleeting sense of calm.

"l know," responds the voice in sorrow.

"Can you help us?" Dave asks.

"I don't know."

"Is there anything you can tell me?" Dave asks.

"Yes," the voice replies, wearily.

"What?" Dave asks, calm giving way to anxiety.

"Angelique's spirit has passed," she says. "Do not fear to put her body to rest. Only Allander's soul resides in the body."

The wind picks up.

"Is there anything else?" Dave asks.

"I must go before something evil is attracted to our meeting." Her voice is sadness itself. A slight image of Amy can be seen hovering between the table and balcony railing.

"No," Dave cries. "You can't go. I can't stay here alone, without you. I'm going back home."

"No" Amy's apparition appears to sigh. "You won't. And this I know, because without you here, you and the others would meet the same end I did. It is time for me to leave." She fades away without fanfare, as quietly as she arrived.

"No!" Dave cries, tears springing to his eyes.

Just then, Jacob Allander's spirit can be seen beyond the balcony's edge.

"Leave her be," he says, "or her eternal soul shall be vanquished!"

"Fuck you!" Dave shouts.

All of the candles go out as Dave and the ghost are left in the pale light of the waxing moon. Allander passes through the balcony railing, approaching Dave.

"Stay back," Dave says. "I'm warning you!" Allander grasps Dave by the hair and pulls his head back, almost tenderly. "No," Dave whispers. He begins to faint.

"You will be mine when the time comes," Allander promises. "I shall take your body next."

Allander lets go of Dave and his limp body slumps to the balcony floor. Allander smiles… and vanishes.

Chapter 44

Three men and two women are sitting around a table in one of the cabins at the village. Candles light the room.

One of the men speaks.

"We've always trusted Ránulf and Rowan before," he says.

"But *something* is going on at that house!" one woman says.

"Before, we could go up to the house whenever we pleased," the second man speaks. "Now, they don't even read to the children."

"It's because of Rowena and Geoff's passing," the other woman says. "They are still in mourning and want privacy in the house."

"You know that is bull," says the last man. "Things would continue if Rowena and Geoff had died of natural causes. Whatever is going on at that house is responsible for their deaths."

"I can't believe that!" the first man says. "I just won't accept the idea of Ránulf, Rowan, or Theena doing anything evil."

"But what about those two kids, Dave and Amy?" the first woman asks. "Who the hell are they and what are they doing up there?"

"Dave is to be Ránulf's newest student," the other woman says. "I don't know for sure about Amy, but I heard she may go work in the store in town."

"Speaking of town, what about those last few slayings?" the third man asks. "There have been exactly thirteen murders. No... fifteen, I guess." He picks up a section of the *Omaha World Herald* newspaper from the table. "Six adults and nine children. A hatchet seems to be the weapon of choice."

"Do the police have any leads?" the second guy asks.

"Yes," the third one volunteers. "The persons of interest are Ránulf, Rowan, and Matt. Or anybody else from the covenstead."

"I think it's time we talk to Ránulf directly," the first man concludes.

Chapter 45

A man with long, black hair sits in a leather easychair before a fireplace. He is thought to be the most evil living man in this part of the country. This was the man who took Jacob Allander's place in the Allander Cult. The cult is now called The Church of Nyarlathotep's Reign. They no longer center their worship on the Christian god, Satan, but on multiple dark gods from all the world's religions. This man, the leader of this evil coven is Kim Batchons. He does not compete with Ránulf Wylkyn, nor does he care what Ránulf or his witches do with themselves. Ránulf, however, keeps a close eye on Batchons.

Kim is reading *The Witching Hour* by Anne Rice, enjoying the escapism of the historical and gothic details. But, something causes him to raise his eyes up from his book.

The doorbell rings.

His wife is asleep so he gets up to go to the door. *Who would ring the doorbell at five in the morning?* he wonders.

He opens the door, and to his surprise, a small girl dressed quite eloquently, but with an old stocking cap stands before him.

"Hello," she says in a sweet voice.

Kim steps back. *Something is wrong.*

"Who are you?" Kim asks.

"Angelique," she says and smiles.

Kim mentally casts a protective sphere around himself.

"What do you want?"

"I have a message from your master," Angelique says, cryptically.

"I have no master," Kim says as he begins to close the door.

Angelique pushes the door open in an instant, knocking Kim to the ground. Kim quickly recovers and hops back up, a sense of dread finally emerging from his, thus far, cautionary approach to this situation.

"You have the eyes of the possessed!" Kim cries.

"That I do, Kim Batchons." Angelique smiles. "And if you cooperate, I won't have to possess *you*."

Kim reaches into his shirt and exposes a medallion.

"Stay back, fiend," Kim threatens.

"Whatever could be wrong, Batchons?" Angelique asks. "Are you not the master of all evil?"

Several objects in the room begin to levitate as the door slams shut.

Kim touches his medallion.

"Nyarlathotep," he whispers. "Azathoth and Cthulhu." The objects fall from the air.

"What spirits are those that protect you?" Angelique cries. "Satan stands behind me!"

"Satan?" Kim says with a laugh. "The Christian god of stupidity? One of his spirits cannot possibly threaten me."

"You have brought me shame!" Angelique rages. "The Cult of Allander follows none but Satan!"

Kim's face pales.

"The Cult of Allander is no more," he whispers. "For Satan is humbled before *my* gods."

Angelique screams in rage, shattering all of the glass in Kim's home, including the center of Kim's medallion.

"Your shield is gone, Batchons," Angelique growls. "Contact with your gods is no more! I am Jacob Allander, fool, and Satan will destroy you!"

Violet fire erupts around Angelique as Kim gasps.

"Allander?" he asks.

Angelique's eyes go to the back of her head as she raises her flaming hands. The fire turns from purple to the darkest red.

"Your punishment shall forever be in Satan's Hell!" she screams. The red fire pours forth from her spread fingers to surround Kim just as he raises his own arms.

"Yog-Soggoth!" Kim cries. "Expel this minion of the lesser demon from my home! Bathe the possessed in your ever evil! Show Allander why he is no more!"

Angelique's red flames extinguish immediately as a sonic boom shakes the house. She is thrown to the ground as an enormous pressure begins to smash her. The floor groans beneath her.

"Your time is past!" Kim cries as he continues to channel the crushing pressure onto Angelique. She cries out in pain and fear. Smoke starts to fly from her darkening skin.

"No!" With effort, she momentarily pulls free of the spell and curses at Kim. "Bitch dog!"

Barely pulling free, Allander flees in Angelique's body.

"Why won't it snow?" Allander cries as he rushes into the street. Angelique's flesh is quite charred and her body is crying for *nutrition*. She runs across the street and around the back of the house there, startling a large racoon near the garbage bins. It screeches and nips at her ankles. She reaches down with preternatural strength and grabs the animal, biting directly into its face. Within five minutes, only the fur, skin, and bones are left.

Angelique returns to Kim's home. A strong psychic shield surrounds it.

"Fuck," Angelique mutters. "This guy could kick Ránulf's ass." Angelique raises her arms and concentrates on an upstairs_window. Slowly, she opens a void in Kim's psychic shield.

Kim is alert in his own bedroom. He can sense the tear in his shield. He goes to the door of his wife's room. She hadn't emerged throughout the recent racket downstairs.

Outside, Angelique is pleased to see the face of Kim Batchons' wife looking out of her bedroom window. Allander's spirit is even more thrilled to see Kim's wife crashing through the window and landing in the partially melted snow of the front yard, breaking her neck, wrist, and spine.

Kim throws open the door to his wife's room and runs to the window.

"Bethany!" Kim cries. He sees Angelique fleeing the house.

That afternoon, after the circus of police, reporters, and window-repair contractors had wrapped up, Kim sat again in his leather chair. Somehow, he was bested by Allander in those early morning hours and retribution was primary in his mind. He casually chases 2 tablets of amphetamine sulfate with a deep swallow of brandy. He began to recall the events surrounding the death of Jacob Allander. He was shot by police and dragged a baby to death with him. Kim was there and witnessed the whole thing. He was nineteen at the time. Unknown to anyone, Kim was the one who informed Ránulf about the planned sacrifice that night. Kim disliked Jacob Allander. He disliked his views on religion and he disliked his sentiments about evil. How could Allander be back now? Especially if he's only backed by a dying Christian god? He thought briefly about getting in contact with Ránulf. A communing session with one of his gods would help. Surely, one of Nyarlathotep's 999 forms would give him acceptable advice.

The next day Rowan, Theena, and Matt awake within half an hour of each other. They find Ránulf and Dave already gone. Rowan ventures outside with Matt for some fresh air.

"Amy's body has been removed," Matt says as they are walking. "That was the worst thing I think I will ever have to do in my life."

"I wish this could all be over," Rowan says, sighing. His exhaustion has settled into his bones. "If Ránulf is hurt or worse, I don't think I could successfully replace him. Plus, the village witches are getting agitated about the house being restricted."

"It has to be," Matt says. "None of them can be here in case something else happens, or someone else is killed."

Rowan looks into the silent sky.

"That's weird," he says, puzzled. "Where are my ravens? They always are around when I'm outside."

"You must remember," Matt says, "that the creatures all have their own free will."

Rowan caws, mimicking the sound of the ravens. Yet, they do not come.

"To tell you the truth," Rowan says, "I haven't noticed them since Timbre died."

"I haven't seen Bast, either," Matt realizes.

Meanwhile, Dave is still unconscious, lying on the third floor's balcony patio. The ravens are all lined-up on the railing. Bast appears on the balcony and approaches Dave. She looks at the ravens and meows. They all take to the sky, cawing, as Bast snuggles up against Dave's chest.

As Rowan and Matt are returning, Rowan sees the ravens flying above the house. They fly above him and land on nearby trees.

"They were behind the house," Rowan says.

Matt and Rowan hurry to the rear of the house.

"Nothing here," Matt says.

The ravens return to the balcony, and are once again chased off by Bast.

"Maybe we should check the balcony," Matt suggests. They go in the back door and up to the third floor. Rowan throws open the balcony door and is shocked to see Bast lying atop Dave, who is unconscious. Bast gets up, stretches, and runs into the house.

Matt and Rowan lift Dave and take him into his room.

"Matt," Rowan says, "can you find Theena and ask her to bring her healing bag? I'm going to see what he was doing out on the balcony all night."

Matt runs downstairs, as Rowan goes upstairs and back out to the balcony. Rowan sees the extinguished candles and the book, *Ghost Spells*. He thinks that after dabbling with necromancy, there is a decent chance Dave could awaken possessed. He grabs the book and that is when he notices Amy's coat. He takes it and goes back to Dave's room. Theena and Matt come in at that moment. Theena takes a sachet of herbs from her bag and places it under Dave's nose. He moans and begins to awaken.

"Shit," he mumbles as he sits up. A wave of dizziness hits him and he lies right back down.

"I don't think he's possessed," Rowan observes.

"Why would he be?" Theena asks with a raised brow.

Rowan holds up *Ghost Spells* and Amy's coat.

"He was summoning spirits last night," he says.

"I'm okay," Dave mumbles. He sits up, slowly this time.

"What happened to you?" Matt asks.

"I was trying to get Amy to help us," he replies.

"You shouldn't mess around with the supernatural, Dave," Theena says. "You're not experienced enough."

From downstairs, the telephone rings. Rowan proceeds down to answer it.

"Hello?" he says into the receiver.

"May I please speak with Ránulf? It's urgent," the voice on the other end says.

"I'm afraid he's not here right now," Rowan says. "Would you like to leave a message? Or, maybe I can help you?"

"This is Kim Batchons," the voice says.

Rowan's face turns a ghostly shade.

"Oh," Rowan says, flatly. "What can I help *you* with?"

"I need to speak to you or Wylkyn in person," Kim says. "Can you come to my house and have Ránulf arrive once he's available?"

"When?" Rowan asks.

"Now."

"Well," Rowan says, hesitantly, "it would probably be best if I waited for Ránu—"

"It's about Allander," Kim interrupts.

"I'll be over," Rowan says and hangs up the phone.

Theena comes downstairs.

"Who was it, Rowan?"

"Kim Batchons," Rowan says. "He has some information on Allander that could help. I'm going over to his house."

Theena gasps.

"No, you are not ! That man is evil and I'm not letting you go over there. At least wait for Ránulf!"

"I don't even know where Ránulf is. I can't wait for him," Rowan argues.

"I know I won't talk you out of it," Theena says, "and there is *no way* I am going over there so at least take Matt or Dave."

"No," he says, shaking his head. "I can't do that. It's too risky."

"Be careful, then," Theena says and leans forward to kiss him.

Elsewhere, Ránulf is walking in the forest with his familiar, the black buck. No words exchange between them, but the meaning of their thoughts are quite clear to one another. Another death on the covenstead would destroy it. The presence of police would finally hit critical mass and there surely would be a federal investigation. The very worst is that the witches would begin to leave and everything they had built here would be lost.

Rowan's ravens silently perch themselves in the trees surrounding Ránulf. Ránulf can tell that danger is awaiting Rowan in the form of Angelique. Her growth rate is quite accelerated. When Allander first possessed her, she was but an infant, just becoming a toddler. Now, she has the physical attributes of a second-grader. It's not unknown, though, for the body of a host to advance while under diabolic possession.

He remembers back to the night of Allander's death. Winter solstice, 1977. Kim Batchons had revealed to him Allander's plans to carry out the sacrifice. Even if the events went without interruption, Allander would have had to face the fact that "Satan" would not appear. His nonexistence assured him of that. *Don't all gods exist?* he wondered for the umpteenth time. *In the souls of their worshippers? Surely there is room in the cosmic subconscious of humankind for all our gods. Be they Celtic, Norse, Egyptian, Greek, Roman, Islamic, Jewish, African, or Christian?* These thoughts always battled each other in Ránulf's mind. Of course, he believed that his own gods guided, not created, the evolution of humans and the Earth. Thus, other gods were powerless in that sense. *Best to not think about it. I'm too old. And I could be wrong.* He walks back to the manor.

Rowan knocks on Kim Batchons' door. Kim's newest harlot allows Rowan to enter the house.

"Greetings, Rowan," Kim says frantically. "I'm glad you could come."

"Well met," Rowan greets him.

"Please," Kim ushers him to a sofa. "Sit."

The harlot brings tea to Rowan and Kim.

"It's herbal," Kim says, grimacing. "Don't worry. I am perfectly prepared to tolerate your beliefs while you are here."

"Thank you?" Rowan offers. *Are my beliefs summed up with Bigelow tea bags?* he wondered.

"Calling you was a gamble on my part," Kim admits. "I did not know if you knew of Jacob's current state."

"Yes." Rowan sets his tea down. "Ránulf and I are aware of Allander's return to the realm of the living and his possession of Angelique Barker."

"Who was she?" Kim asks.

"No one who was chosen for any particular qualities," Rowan says evasively. "She was just the most convenient being for

Allander to possess before the thaw."

"Before the thaw?" Kim asks, confused.

"Before Angelique," Rowan says, then pauses, "Allander was trapped in the form of a snowman."

Kim laughs, not sure himself if in uneasiness or amusement.

"You must be kidding," he says, then sees no irony in Rowan's face, convincing him immediately of its truth.

"He returned to this world on December 21st, the winter solstice," Rowan says.

Kim nods. "The thirteenth anniversary of his death."

"Allander has caused approximately fifteen deaths," Rowan informs him.

"Sixteen," Kim says, darkly. "Though it is documented as suicide, my beloved wife was killed yesterday morning."

"Tell me about it," Rowan says.

"At 5:00 AM a small girl in a white dress rang my doorbell," Kim says.

"She was wearing an odd stocking cap, too. She said she had a message from my master. When I denied having a master, she forced her way in. That's when I could tell she was possessed. It was in her eyes. She was enraged that the Cult of Allander no longer existed as before."

He paused a beat, then continued.

"Then I said something mocking Satan and she got pissed *bad*!" he says laughing. "She claimed to be Jacob Allander. Then, she... she engulfed me in this red fire—"

He pauses again, this time to catch his breath.

"I managed to drive her… him… out, using my own gifts of the Art. Naturally, I immediately cast a psychic aura protecting my home, but it was opened and Allander drew my Bethany through the window to her death."

"Anything since then?" Rowan asks.

"Just little annoyances," Kim says. "Howling last night, rattling at the windows. For the most part, I have accepted the aid of various deities to protect me. But, it's the dream I had. It was so lucid. I only remember that Wylkyn and I were humbled before Jacob Allander's incarnation. A voice told me to get Wylkyn's aid. So, I called. And here *you* are."

"You say deities are protecting you," Rowan says. "Then why call? What exactly do you fear?"

"My home is my haven," Kim says, sighing. "But outside these walls I am afraid to venture. I figure that together we can put Allander back in the grave. Ridding a host of a demon or spirit is not that difficult."

"It's not that simple," Rowan says. "The item which links Allander to our world is the hat which Angelique was wearing. It must be destroyed."

"How is the hat connected to this?" Kim asks, baffled.

"From what Ránulf said," Rowan says, thinking back, "Allander evacuated his soul into the dying baby. The infant's mother took the baby out into the snow, using the hat to gently stop the baby's bleeding. The baby and the mother both died in the snow."

"That's why Allander came back as a snowman?" Kim asks. "How ludicrous!"

"Ránulf has prepared a ritual which will summon Allander," Rowan informs Kim. "We think it is possible that Allander's spirit can temporarily leave Angelique's body. His spirit attacked a friend who was trying to talk to the spirit of his girlfriend."

"I've got it!" Kim stands up. "If we can trap Angelique's body, Wylkyn can summon Allander and leave Angelique undefended. We take the hat and destroy it."

"That may work," Rowan says, "but I think we should let Ránulf draft the final plan."

"And I will!" Ránulf says, walking into the room.

"Where did you come from?" Kim demands.

"Thy bathroom, lad, I really had to go." Ránulf smiles.

"How can we be sure you are Ránulf?" Kim asks, his anger beginning to show.

"Who else would I be?" Ránulf asks. "I am Ránulf, I assure ye."

"How did you get into my house?" Kim asks, his confusion showing. "I would've known if you crossed my psychic alarm."

"And so would've Allander," Ránulf says. "He is closer than thee'd like, I'd wager, just waiting for ye to step outside."

Kim pales and sits down.

"That's better," Ránulf says. "Now how did ye say you ridded thyself of Angelique?"

"I summoned a spell of *spellturning*, which dissipated Allander's fire," Kim says. "Then I channeled a *banishment* incantation from the Old Ones, hoping to banish Allander back to the spirit plane; but all the demon did was flee."

"Aye," Ránulf says. "For some reason most spells which affect ghosts and the undead are not effective against Allander. We are lucky that the weather is on our side, for if it snows, the snowman will return. In that form, Allander is most elusive."

"Normal invisibility and dimming spells do not fool undead,

correct?" Rowan asks.

"Right," Kim says, "but there are spells which can make you specifically invisible to spirits and the like."

"Aye," Ránulf agrees, "but I gather they are ineffective, no? Necromancy is Mr. Batchons' field of specialty, is it not?"

"Allander's spirit is too independent to be normally ensnared or controlled," Kim says. "Banishment is also only temporary. I gather that he hasn't tried to use very many spells?"

"Of course!" Ránulf realizes in excitement. "No wonder his ghost is so strong! His spells have changed. As a snowman, he can create and command ice."

"But it's not real ice," Rowan kicks in.

"The ice in our kitchen was quasi-real.," Ránulf says. "It was part illusion, part reality."

"Shadow magic?" Kim asks.

"Aye," Ránulf confirms. "Shadow magic. It looks real and is real to the five senses, but is only partially there in this dimension."

As Ránulf, Rowan, and Kim continue their conversation, Angelique is relaxing in someone's home.

"Yes!" she cries. "*Dark Shadows* is back on the air!" Her eyes roll to their whites as she opens her mouth, exposing fangs. She hisses like a vampire, then falls into a fit of giggling.

A man and woman enter through the front door.

"Oh my goodness!" the woman cries out. "Who are you, little girl?"

"What's your name?" the man demands.

"Uhhhh..." Angelique gives them a guilty look. "Angie."

"I think we will have to call your parents, young lady," the woman says.

"Honestly," the man says with a sigh. "Breaking into someone's house to watch television!"

"Oh shut up!" Angelique says. "You bore me."

"My!" the woman exclaims. "Young lady, you leave right now before we go fetch the law."

"Fetch this, bitch," Allander's voice commands from Angelique's mouth.

The curtains rip themselves from the windows and entwine around the woman. She screams. The man freezes in place.

"Lonnie!" he cries.

"Silence, you ass," Allander says. Black tendrils whip forth from Angelique's fingers and surround the man. They make contact, suction onto his face and body, and he implodes into nothingness. Angelique gestures at the curtains and says, "Shatter."

The window shatters, but the glass shards remain hovering in the air. Then, they quickly dart toward the woman, embedding into her flesh. A second pulse runs through them and the shards all simultaneously vibrate further into her body. Her cries of death are music to Allander's ears.

"Goodbye... Lonnie!" Allander taunts.

Suddenly, Angelique stops, her eyes darting around the room, looking for something, or someone. She raises her arms and closes her eyes with the intention of detecting scrying. Her fears are validated as her spell signals that she is indeed being spied upon.

"A *false vision* spell would do nicely, here," Angelique mutters, and prepares an illusion to send back to the nosy scryer.

Ránulf and Rowan are chanting while Kim momentarily leaves the room. Ránulf casts a scrying spell for Angelique to discover her whereabouts, but how weird! At first Angelique was in a nearby living room, but then the vision changed. Angelique was marching steadily toward Batchons' house.

"Batchons!" Ránulf exclaims. "Allander is coming!"

Rowan goes to a window. "Where is she?"

Kim Batchons comes into the room.

"How do you know?" he asks.

"I used a scrying spell," Ránulf says.

"Scrying can be altered by the one you are scrying on," Kim says. "Cover me."

Kim dons a black trenchcoat and steps outside into the cold day. His hands gesture in a complicated pattern as he breathily sighs a mystical phrase. He detects an undead presence in a home about two blocks away.

"Your scrying attempt *was* foiled, Ránulf," he comes back inside to say. "Allander is in a house about two blocks from here."

Rowan looks back outside.

"It's supposed to get cold again," he says. The first flurries begin to fall as his brow creases in worry.

"Well, Batchons," Ránulf says, "I'm afraid we cannot stay with ye much longer. Will ye be okay alone?"

"You have got to be kidding, Wylkyn!" Kim cries. "Allander is mere blocks from here! When you leave, he comes. You are not leaving!"

Suddenly, a siren-like sound deafens Kim, Rowan, and Ránulf. Kim and Rowan fall to the floor as Ránulf realizes that the spell isn't affecting him as much. He mutters a dispelling incantation and the sound stops. Ránulf cradles Rowan's ears and his hands glow a light green.

"Better?" Ránulf asks.

"Yes," Rowan says, holding his ears. "A little. Thank you."

Kim manages to pull himself together.

"What was that?" Rowan asks.

"A *deafness* spell," Kim mutters, then looks at Ránulf. "Why didn't it affect *you*?"

"Allander is blind to me bein' here," Ránulf explains. "I reckon he cast for two, Rowan and yerself."

"But how could Allander cast the spell if he's not even here?" Rowan asks.

"Wylkyn… Ránulf…" Kim interrupts, "now you must let me come with you. If you won't stay then I must seek refuge on your estate!"

"Nay," Ránulf says with a frown. "That would but worsen the image of my witches if ye were there. However, I do not think Allander will be bothering ye anytime soon despite this last spell."

With that cryptic remark, Ránulf and Rowan leave.

Chapter 46

Matt, Dave, and Theena have completed Amy's burial in the small estate cemetery.

"It's beginning to snow," Theena says, softly.

"I have this overwhelming sense of doom," Matt says. "Like something is going to happen very soon."

The three of them walk back to the house to find that Rowan is home.

"Where's Ránulf?" Dave asks.

"He went for a walk before it gets dark," Rowan says while stir-frying vegetables. "But he left something for you on his desk in his room."

In his room? Dave wonders. He goes upstairs and approaches Ránulf's room. It is locked; but as he fumbles with the knob, it opens. Dave walks into the room. It is lit with four beeswax pillar candles. The door closes by itself behind him. The room is L-shaped with a spiral staircase in one corner. He hadn't quite clocked it his last time here, but he makes the connection on how the room is connected to the first floor and basement. Dave approaches Ránulf's desk. A scrolled parchment lies on the desk with a flask and some incense. Dave picks up the scroll and unwraps it. It is a message from Ránulf.

David,

I have reason to believe thy essence is unclean, for thy aura has been tainted by thy contact with Allander last night. Ignite the incense on this desk. Meditate on your soul being flooded with white light and purity. Then, drink the contents of this flask. It will protect ye from possible possession or abduction by Allander, if I fail to contain him.

—R

"Fail to contain him?" Dave whispers. He compartmentalizes the thought as he sets the note back on the desk. He lights the incense and strips naked. He sits on the floor, cross-legged, stretching each foot to rest on top of each thigh.

This hurts, he thinks. He tries to clear his mind and breathes in the incense. Its purifying scent begins to excite him, but he ignores his hardening seedstick. He visualizes his body bathed in cleansing, white light. Almost immediately he feels Allander's influence leaving him. He drinks the syrupy, bittersweet liquid from the flask.

As he manually uncrosses his legs, his hand brushes his erect penis. A shock of unexpected pleasure grips Dave as he exhales heavily with a moan.

I think this incense has some lust-inducing properties as well as purifying, he thinks. He stands up and looks around Ránulf's room again. He laughs as he sees a picture on a shelf of a semi-clad woman exposing her breasts.

Distracted, Dave extinguishes the incense. The need to beat-off was almost overwhelming. He quickly dressed, adjusting his uncomfortable erection. He snuffs out the candles with his fingers and leaves.

Theena and Rowan are in Theena's room. Ránulf thought they should have separate rooms because everyone needs their privacy but their bedrooms were right next to each other, allowing use of the door connecting their rooms.

"The snow is starting to get worse," Theena says.

"I hope Ránulf hurries and finishes what he's doing," Rowan says. "I have a protective aura around the house so we'll know if Allander enters, but I'm not up to fighting him."

"Where is Ránulf?" Theena asks. "I mean, what's he doing?"

"He's out in the woods," Rowan replies.

"Doing what, though?"

"Theena, don't pry. You know how he is. He just said he'd be busy."

"I do know how he is," Theena says. "Under the circumstances, though, a little transparency would help me feel a bit better prepared."

Ránulf is sitting in the forest. The snow is not yet collecting on the ground. Arcane figures are carved into the dirt. Two incense burners are releasing a spirit-summoning scent into the air. He has a very thick book in front of him, *The Daemon Witche.*

"Allander!" Ránulf stands and bellows. "I summon thee!"

The possessed body of Angelique is quickly approaching Kim Batchons' front door. She stops.

"No," she whispers deeply in Allander's voice. "Let me be, Ránulf." She raises her arms and mutters a foreign curse. Violet flames erupt from her.

Ránulf stands in the forest, halted in his spell by violet flames which erupt around him. He dismisses the flames and again tries to summon Allander to his waiting circle.

Kim Batchons puts down his book. Something is nearing the psychic aura surrounding his home. He goes to a window facing the street in front of the house.

"Allander!" he cries, hoarsely. *Damn Ránulf for leaving!* he thinks. Then, *I am not going down without a fight.* He grabs a staff and an ornate dagger from his study.

Angelique steps onto Kim's small, open front porch.

"Ohhhh, Batchons!" Angelique taunts.

"Allander!" comes Ránulf's voice again, louder, shattering Allander's hold on Angelique's body.

Allander screams through Angelique's body as he is torn from it to appear before Ránulf.

The body of Angelique is thrown through Kim's front door, reducing it to splinters.

The circle before Ránulf is surrounding a triangle with three equal sides, also carved into the ground.

Then, where nothing was a moment before, the spectre of Jacob Allander stands in the center of the triangle.

"Greetings, Ránulf," Allander says, "you decaying old bastard."

"Allander," Ránulf says, nodding.

"You can't hold me in this sideshow wizard's geometry forever," Allander says.

"I needn't," Ránulf agrees. "Batchons is doing what I expect of him."

When Kim's front door exploded, he began to rapidly call on his evil gods to aid him. But, he quickly realized the body of Angelique was not moving. Reaching out with his hidden senses, he determined that Allander's presence had left her and that the plan was underway.

Back in the forest, Ránulf sits, watchful of the trapped shade of Allander who continues to taunt him.

"Nay tha's not got hold on me, Allander," Ránulf says, harshly. "Ye may as well cease trying."

"How terribly sad that I can cast no spells inside this circled triangle," Allander mourns, falsely. "Especially if I had a host body, Ránulf, I could give you immortality and the secrets of death!"

"I *know* the secrets of death, Jacob Allander," Ránulf says. "And I need no gifts from ye."

"Damn you!" Allander howls. "I am going to slay you! Release me from this prison."

Ránulf chuckles.

"You don't know all the secrets of death, Ránulf," Allander says, calmly. "Otherwise you would know why, and how I am here. You would know how it was possible for me to return."

"Aye," Ránulf says. "I may not know all the secrets of death, but it's not for thee to know why *I'm* standin' here, neither."

"Rowena, Geoff, and Amy were such good kills, Ránulf," Allander taunts. "I bedded all of them before I killed them. I raped their souls!"

"Silence!" Ránulf commands, casting a spell of the same name.

Dismayed, Allander found he could not speak. Even more dismayed, he discovered his telepathic and telekinetic powers would not function while he was trapped in this circle. Now was not the time to argue with Ránulf anyway. *Now* was the time to free himself from this mystical trap. He had to concentrate on the hat. The snow was coming down hard now, but not inside of Ránulf's or his circles. The hat was his connection to this world. So was the snow. He must get free of Ránulf's prison!

At the manor, the doorbell rings. Theena gets up to answer it as Rowan and Dave are talking. Matt is at the village going about his regular duties.

Theena opens the door and gasps in alarm.

Immediately, Rowan stands up, sensing danger. Kim Batchons pushes past Theena into the house.

"Rowan," he says, gruffly, "where is Ránulf?"

"He is out," Rowan says. "You were told that you were not welcome here."

"I think this will change your mind," Kim says. From inside of his trenchcoat he pulls out the snowman's hat.

Dave gasps and Theena utters a cry.

"How?" Dave asks. "Who are you?"

"I am Kim Batchons, young man," Kim replies, glaring. Dave

is shocked. Of course he had heard of Ránulf's nationwide news, but he had heard of Kim Batchons, too. The worst thing is that a few years ago, Kim was rumored to have moved to Kansas City, Missouri, but now he is in Omaha? He is supposed to be the leader of the largest Satanic cult in this part of the country, maybe the whole United States. He even has followers in Canada, but he is rivaled in Europe, so he stays away from there. Kim is said to be behind so many crimes and to even have influence within the government. Naturally, no one can prove anything. Then again, how much of this was just the narrative of a great PR team? How on Earth, though, did he get the hat? Was he behind Allander's return?

"I know what you are thinking," Kim says to Dave, "and I am not behind Allander's return. I am no danger to any of you, either. I just need to get this hat to Ránulf."

"So Ránulf was able to force Allander out of Angelique's body?" Rowan asks.

"That is what I assume," Kim says.

"Then let's destroy the hat," Theena says. They all travel to the basement and light the fire in the utility room. Rowan goes into the room with the circle to open a cabinet in the altar. He pulls out a bowl of salt and the sharpest athame he can find. He then goes into Ránulf's lab and finds a vial of a consecrated oil, which he knows to be flammable.

Rowan goes back into the utility room and sees that Theena has lit some sacred incense.

"Let's get this over with," Kim says.

Dave has gotten the fire raging. Rowan takes the hat from Kim, just barely closing himself off to the evil it contains. He takes the purifying oil and begins to soak some into the hat.

In the forest, Allander has stopped trying to free himself. He figures he can outwait Ránulf. Suddenly, a stinging, purifying feeling hits him. Allander cries out, powerful enough to break Ránulf's *silence* spell.

"The hat!" Allander cries. "Someone is purifying the hat!" He looks at Ránulf in despair. "You cannot do this!" He begins to struggle against his prison in earnest.

On the road to Ránulf's house, an undercover police car, containing two detectives, waits.

One is a woman, the other a man. The woman finishes talking on her radio. "We were right, Douglas," she says. "The plates on that last car say it belongs to Kim Batchons."

"So that means he is in league with Ránulf as we expected?" Douglas asks.

"That's what the facts say," she says. "We should probably take advantage of that search warrant before another murder occurs."

She starts the car and begins the drive up Ránulf's driveway. Along the way, several snowmen beside the drive stare lifelessly at the two detectives.

"Someone has been busy making these snowmen," Douglas remarks.

"Yeah," the woman says, "but why do they all look so pissed?"

They approach Ránulf's parking area and see Kim Batchons' car.

"I think we'll search that one, first," Douglas says. They kill the engine and step out into the falling snow. Dusk is quickly falling. Douglas opens the door to Kim's car.

"The asshole doesn't even lock his doors, Anne," he says.

Anne goes over and looks in. The keys are still in the ignition.

"How convenient," she mumbles. She takes the keys and approaches the trunk while Douglas searches the inside of the car.

Sighing, she fits the key in the trunk's keyhole. She opens it and calls for Douglas. He comes over and they both stare at a covered body.

Anne begins to lift the sheet. Under it is the lifeless body of Angelique.

"Call it in," Anne says.

Back in the utility room, Rowan tries to cut the hat. It is proving to be unnaturally resilient.

"Forget it," Dave says. "Let's just burn the goddamn thing."

Rowan takes a deep breath and throws it into the fire.

A deafening howl erupts from the forest. The witches at the village all stop what they are doing. Many of them confront Matt and it is decided that he will take two villagers with him and go into the forest to search for the source of the howl. The two detectives look towards the forest, also. Douglas runs for the radio and nearly shits his pants when he finds that all he can get from it is static.

"Shit!" Anne exclaims. "We'll have to take this body in ourselves." They begin to transport it to their vehicle.

Rowan, Kim, Theena, and Dave all hear the howl from inside the basement. Luckily for them, with the addition of the oil, the hat starts to burn. They all sigh their relief. A void opens where the hat is burning, but the hat continues to burn. Spirits of the dead begin to rush out of the void. Rowan and Theena both make hand symbols to turn away the undead. Many of the spectres flee back into the void, faced with this magic. Kim casts a spell to hold the undead in their place, preventing the spirits from exiting their void.

The hat, despite the tear between the worlds, burns to completion. After it is consumed, the void swallows the fire and vanishes. In the forest, the spectre of Allander is screaming, despite Ránulf's attempts at another *silence* spell.

"Be silent now, Allander," Ránulf demands. "Ye can return to the dead for your earthly connection has been destroyed!"

"Destroying me isn't as simple as only destroying the hat!" Allander cries. He calms and laughs to himself.

"I will no longer be held here," he says. With his last reserve of energy, he destroys the imprisoning triangle around him. Yet, he is still trapped in the circle.

Ránulf stands up with urgency.

"By all the gods, I command thee—remain within that circle!" he screams at Allander. Out of desperation he casts a spell to control the dead.

Allander laughs.

"Try as you may, Ránulf," he says, laughing slowly and deliberately, "but I shall soon be free and your death will arrive."

Ránulf diverts his attention internally and attempts to send a telepathic message to Rowan to request his aid.

At the house, Rowan tells the others to get their coats on.

"We have to go into the forest and find Ránulf," he says. He goes to the library and gets the disk for fire. Then, they all go out the back door into the heavily falling snow, and start off toward the forest.

Detectives Anne and Douglas have set Angelique's body in the trunk of their vehicle as carefully as possible. They get in and Anne starts the car.

"Who do you think she is?" Anne asks.

"Probably one of his harlots," Douglas says. "Someone to replace his latest wife."

"What happened to her?" Anne asks.

"She took a leap from her window," Douglas says.

Ránulf is still with Allander.

"I *will* be free!" Allander cries.

"Shut tha gob," Ránulf says. "Ye shall not be free so long as I stand here."

"Then maybe *'ye'* need a distraction," Allander says as he raises his hands. "Satan, lend me your strength. Allow your demonic influence to free me from this prison! Lucifer, hear me! Dispel this circle and slay the wizard!"

The wind begins to pick up, and yet nothing happens.

"Master!" Allander cries. "Forsake me not! Free me!"

"I see thy 'master' is a very prompt entity," Ránulf mocks.

"Mock not Satan!" Allander rages. All at once Allander cries out and channels all his being into dismissing the rest of the circle that holds him. Unfortunately for Ránulf, Allander is released.

"Now it is time for you to die!" Allander cries with lusty vengeance. He approaches the circle which protects Ránulf.

"Aye, I reckon not," Ránulf mutters, calm as stone. He calls upon his gods. "Banish this spectre to where death does dwell. Return him to his make-shift hell."

Electric-blue light erupts around Ránulf as he finishes his spell to banish Allander's shade. He does not stop with the one casting, but begins to also complete a working to dispel evil.

"Dispel this evil shade from me. Turn him round and he shall flee," he commands as white light issues from his hands toward

Allander.

Allander screams as both the *banish* and *dispel evil* spells strike him. Then, there is silence in the forest. Allander is gone.

Rowan and the others approach Ránulf.

"Why did you banish him?" Kim asks. "There's not much he can do unless he inhabits a body."

"Those spells shall weaken him so he cannot take any bodies," Ránulf says. "Possibly for a couple of days."

"His hat is destroyed," Theena informs him.

"Aye," Ránulf says. "But what news o' Angelique?"

"She is in the trunk of my car," Kim says.

"Nay," Ránulf contradicts him. "An owl just recently told me that a man and a woman took a body from the vehicle that belongs to the 'man with the darkness about him'."

"Shit!" Kim exclaims.

"Who was on the estate?" Rowan asks.

"Probably police," Theena mutters.

The five return to the house. Just to verify Ránulf's claims, Kim checks his trunk. It is empty.

Anne and Douglas are racing towards the station.

"The radio's still not working," Douglas curses.

Anne slows down as the roads are getting worse.

"This weather could have something to do with it," she says, concentrating on what's in front of her. As the detectives' car rounds a bend, they unexpectedly encounter a semi lunging at them, driving in the middle of the road.

"Look out!" Douglas wanted to scream, but he couldn't because the car was rolling in the ditch, glass breaking and metal screeching. Eventually, the car stops upside-down. The exhausted semi driver opens his eyes and continues on, trying to stay awake until the Sapp Bros. where he can get a shower and "fresh" coffee. As the wheels stop spinning on the car in the ditch, the trunk pops open, releasing Angeliqués dead body into the falling snow. Anne and Douglas are dead.

Matt and the two witches from the village are in the forest, searching for the source of the demonic howl. Finding nothing, they persuade Matt to go to the house with them so they can confront Ránulf.

"We've been kept in the dark too long," the woman, Teresa, complains.

"Okay," Matt says. "I agree. You villagers should know some of the happenings going on around here."

"Like what?" the man, Joseph, asks.

"Ránulf can explain," Matt answers.

They approach the house. The back door is locked, so they go around to the front. To their surprise, they see Kim Batchons getting into his car to leave.

"Who is that?" Teresa asks. "His aura is the most perverted I've ever witnessed."

"I don't know," Matt says.

"Don't play stupid with us," Joseph says. "That man is Kim Batchons! If anyone sees him here the *Herald* will have a field day with it!"

"Kim Batchons?" Teresa asks, shocked. "I can't believe this!"

"I honestly didn't know!" Matt pleads. "I've never seen him before!"

"We need to see Ránulf, now!" Joseph demands.

They enter through the unlocked front door. Theena and Dave are in the living room.

"Matt, Joe, Teresa!" Theena exclaims. "Merry meet. What brings you?"

"Can it, Theena," Joseph says, nearly spitting. "Get Ránulf down here, now!"

Ránulf enters the room.

"Joseph!" he cries, happily. "How are ye? Why the aggravated look?"

"Why was Kim Batchons here?" Teresa asks.

"You know he can ruin the estate's reputation," Joseph says.

"Just a small bit of business," Ránulf replies, smiling.

"I think you should explain," Joseph says. "When the villagers find out about this, there is going to be a lot of trouble."

"That is why they shall not find out about it," Ránulf says in explanation.

"They have a right to know!" Teresa exclaims. "And we *are* going to tell them."

"Ye shall not be telling anyone about it," Ránulf says, pointing a finger at them, "because ye are both going to *forget*."

Suddenly, the looks on Teresa's and Joseph's faces go blank.

"Hello, Ránulf!" Joseph says in cheer. "How are you?"

"Grand!" Ránulf bellows in response.

"What are we doing here?" Teresa asks.

"Leaving," Ránulf volunteers and ushers them both out the door.

"Ránulf!" Matt says with concern after the door is closed. "You made them forget!"

"I had to," he says with a shrug.

"But, Ránulf," Theena says. "Your own villagers? That is low! When they remember, they will just tell the villagers, anyway!"

"By then," Ránulf says, "I hope to have our problems solved."

"What if the village high priest or high priestess detects the *forget* spell?"

"Then they will come to me personally," Ránulf says, "and I will explain the current events to them. Then, they can decide if the villagers should know."

Meanwhile, Kim is driving into town. Omaha. *One of the more promising cities in the Midwest*, he reflects to himself. He had to see one of his police friends. The arrival of Angelique's body at police HQ must not cause a stir. No one must know it came from him or that he was at Ránulf's estate. Luckily enough, Kim had connections everywhere. If things got too tough, he could pull some of the mayor's strings. But, Kim just wasn't feeling that lucky today.

He pulls into the driveway of a small, brick house. He wasn't supposed to be seen here, but this was an emergency. He gets out of his car and approaches the door. The lights were out. Carney could be asleep, already. It was 11 PM, after all. A *knock* spell would work well here.

Kim bends and twists the fingers of his right hand into an impossible formation. Making a semblance of a fist, he knocks lightly, twice. Almost silently, the door clicks open. He enters and closes the door behind him. Noiselessly, Kim steals into a bedroom. A man and a woman lie naked and asleep under the covers.

Kim approaches the man and leans in close.

"Carney," he whispers. "Carney… wake up."

Carney slowly opens his brown eyes and runs a hand through his light brown hair. He smiles.

"Kim?" he sleepily asks as they embrace.

"Indeed." Kim smiles in return. "But I'm afraid this isn't a social visit."

Carney smiles again and asks, "What do you need?"

"I need to make use of your police connections," Kim says. "A body was taken from my car by two brasses. A man and a woman. About a little after dusk. I was at Ránulf's estate. The whole thing needs to be shut down and shut up. Me being at the estate and the body of the girl."

"Well, what's in it for me?" Carney asks, in a gravelly voice.

"I'm sure we can think of something," Kim answers as he reaches under the blankets and grasps Carney's flaccid cock. It thickens and grows erect in his hand.

"You are a devil," Carney groans in pleasure. Kim removes his clothing and joins Craig Carney on the bed. They engage in a number of sexual activities next to Craig's sleeping wife. After they are spent, they lie embraced. Craig reaches for the bedside telephone to phone police HQ. A few words are spoken and he hangs up.

"It's all taken care of, Kim." He licks a salty taste from his lips.

Craig's wife awakens.

"Oh, Kim?" she says. "I suppose you didn't save any of him for me, did you, Craig?"

"No way, Rebecca," Craig says. "He needed a *really big* favor."

All three laugh.

Around 3 AM, Kim leaves the Carney residence and begins the drive home.

At Ránulf's manor, everyone is asleep.

At Anne and Douglas' crash site, nothing has stirred except the four inches of snow that has fallen since 8 AM.

At police HQ, a crooked officer is searching desperately for any evidence of a body of a girl brought from Ránulf's estate. He radios Anne and Douglas's car, but there is no answer.

Good, he thinks. *Maybe they are dead.*

At the witches' village, all are asleep. All… except the high priest and priestess. Something evil has been happening up at the house the past many days. And now, two witches come back with their auras tainted by a *forget* spell that only Ránulf could have placed on them. Tomorrow, or later today, rather, they are duty-bound to confront him.

Chapter 47

Scene: Morning, the snow is falling slightly. Five inches of snow fell during the night. Theena wakes up, showers, and goes downstairs to prepare a morningfeast. Fuck, if she doesn't love a good breakfast and they have reason to… well, not *celebrate* by any means, but at least breathe easier. Dave gets up and plays a little on his guitar. This awakens Matt, so he goes downstairs to rekindle the fire. Rowan awakens and gazes out the window. The snow is now falling very fast. Not the gorgeous, wet, large fluffs that he loves, but severe, tiny specks of powder. By sight, it looks about two below zero. Other than the falling snow, it is very still outdoors.

Only one thing is awakening in earnest. Only one thing stirs in the snow. One thing that comes to awareness with such a perversion as to threaten sanity. The frozen corpse of Angelique Barker writhes underneath a drift of snow near the wrecked police vehicle. Allander allows his chaotic essence to flow back into Angelique, making her emerge from the now-tainted snow. Angelique's appearance is hideous. Her rotting, half-frozen flesh is now dusky blue and her eyes have clouded completely over. Her hair is frozen and ice hangs from her eyebrows and nose. A cloud of steaming corpse gas erupts from Angelique's decaying mouth as Allander laughs from within her. Allander scampers towards Omaha's city limits. A rendezvous with Kim Batchons is in order.

Kim tries to sleep in, but a sense of urgency awakens him early.

"Autumn!" Kim calls as he gets out of bed.

A tightly-dressed young woman enters.

"Yes?" she asks.

"You may prepare my breakfast now."

Autumn quickly goes down to the kitchen and begins to scramble together Kim's breakfast. She doesn't hear the front door open. She doesn't hear a kitchen drawer open behind her as frozen fingers grope blindly for cutlery. Autumn turns around to see the frigid form of Angelique inserting a carving knife into her. She drops Kim's breakfast.

Kim hears her scream.

"Autumn?" he questions, keeping his voice measured. He opens a drawer in his room and withdraws a black semi-automatic 0.22 pistol.

"Autumn?" he asks. "Are you well?"

"No!" screams Allander/Angelique as he lumbers gracelessly into Kim's room. "She is most definitely *not well*!" He cackles but is abruptly cut off.

Three consecrated bullets puncture Angelique's chest and stomach. Allander screams as the magicked bullets emit their power.

Kim's gun flies from his hand and crashes through a window, hit by a telekinetic blast from Allander.

"Fuck!" Kim shouts.

"Your puny effort at magic weapons won't stop me," Allander says.

Kim throws a glass vial at Angelique's feet. It shatters and an unknown liquid spreads from the floor up Angelique's legs. It emanates a misty vapor which surrounds her.

"Your piss shall not keep me from ending you, either," Allander bellows. The mist begins to swirl around Angelique, forcing her to stop.

Kim runs past her and down into his living room. The door to the outside will not open.

Allander extracts himself from the mist and quickly follows. Kim tosses another vial at Angelique, but gasps when it freezes and fails to break when it hits the ground.

Allander laughs and discharges black lightning at the baffled form of Kim Batchons. Kim cries out and collapses unconscious to the floor. Allander laughs and leaves.

At the same time, Rowan and Dave are discussing various topics as Ránulf enters the library.

"Good morning," Dave says.

"Aye, aye, greetings," Ránulf says hurriedly.

He goes directly to his telephone and dials.

"Blast," Ránulf says as he hangs up "No answer."

"Who were you calling?" Dave asks.

"Kim Batchons." Ránulf sighs. "I know he has police connections, so he couldn't have been apprehended for having Angelique's body. I am concerned that neither him or one of his cult member lasses answered the phone."

In the living room, Matt hears a knock at the door. He opens it to find two detectives, both white males.

"Can I help you?" Matt asks, guardedly.

"Yes," the taller man says. "We must speak with Wylkyn."

"I think he might be busy," Matt says.

"No matter," the other detective says, producing a search warrant. "We'll be here for a while."

"Then come in," Matt says. "Be careful what you touch and knock on any closed doors before you enter. You know what happened the last time our house was searched."

"Yes," the tall detective says. "The City of Omaha is still paying you for that ancient obsidian sculpture that was knocked over, I believe."

"Actually, they paid it off months ago," Matt says. "Ránulf is in the library. If you really need him." Matt goes into the kitchen.

"I take it that the library is this way, Scott," the taller detective says heading toward the correct door.

Inside the library, Ránulf, Rowan, and Dave hear three sharp knocks.

"David, go downstairs," Ránulf commands. The urgency in his voice compels Dave to run downstairs into the herb lab.

"Enter!" Ránulf announces to the door.

Scott Zeber and the taller detective, Brad Weiss, enter the library.

"Hello," they both say in unison.

"Greetings," Ránulf says with a smile. "How might I assist ye?"

"I'm Detective Weiss," Brad says. "This is Detective Zeber."

"We're here to ask you a few questions," Zeber says.

"Have a seat." Ránulf motions to a pew-like bench. Weiss and Zeber sit. "Let's have it, then," he insists.

"Did two plain-clothed detectives enter your home yesterday after 6:00 PM?" asks Weiss.

"Nay," Ránulf says. After some thought he adds, "But I did see a man and a woman get into a car and leave."

"When did you see them?" Weiss asks.

"About 7:30, or maybe 8:00," Ránulf says. "I'm not sure."

"How did you see them?" Weiss asks.

"I had come inside from a jaunt in the woods," Ránulf states. "I heard a car start, looked out the window, and saw a woman get into a car where a man already had. They drove off right down the driveway."

"They didn't enter the house?" Weiss asks.

"I have no idea," Ránulf says. "Not through the front door, but I left the back door unlocked while I was out walking. Why were they here? Why are *you* here?"

"We don't know why they were here," Weiss admits. "The last transmission we received from them came from your driveway. It was a request for the identity of the owner of a license plate number. The owner was Kim Batchons. Was he here?"

"Aye," Ránulf says, "but I was out. He told Rowan that

someone was trying to kill him and he needed my assistance."

"Why not come to the police ?" Zeber asks.

"He said it was a supernatural matter," Rowan answers.

"So Satan's come to take his servant back to Hell with him?" Weiss mumbles.

"Batchons does not worship an entity known as Satan, Mr. Weiss," Ránulf says.

"Yes, yes," Weiss says. "I've heard it all before. My apologies. He's still evil."

"And I agree," Ránulf says. "But I do owe him a favor from long ago."

"You said that their 'last transmission' came from our driveway," Rowan says. "Are they missing?"

"No," Weiss says. "We've already found them. Their car rolled from the highway during last night's storm. They're dead."

"That's awful," Ránulf quietly responds.

"Well," Weiss says, standing up, "we've learned all we can for now. I think we should be going. Thank you, Ránulf."

The two detectives depart.

"So the cops that were here crashed," Rowan says with a groan, resting his face in his hands.

"And Angelique was in the trunk," Ránulf finishes his thought for him. "And I don't think the police found her. Shite! Allander will want revenge on Batchons as much as myself. Fair chance that if Allander was able to reinhabit Angelique, we would find him at Batchons' home."

"Who's next to take over his cult if he dies?" Rowan asks.

"No one I know of," Ránulf replies with a shrug. "It may very well crumble."

Another knock at the front door brings Ránulf and Rowan to the living room. Theena opens the door, allowing in the high priest and priestess of the village.

"Woodlin, Isis, well met," Ránulf greets them.

"Possibly ill met, Rán," Isis responds with a sigh. "Unless you possess some good explanations."

"I was hoping the village would not get involved in this," Ránulf says, "but ye both deserve explanations."

Ránulf takes Isis and Woodlin into the library.

"We are being plagued by the vengeful spirit of Jacob Allander," Ránulf says, simply.

"Jacob Allander?" Woodlin asks. "Why does that name sound familiar?"

"Jacob Allander was Kim Batchons' predecessor. A notorious cult leader," Isis says.

"Allander was shot and killed on the winter solstice thirteen years ago," Ránulf explains. "He returned in the form of a possessed, animated snowman. The two young people whom you have seen, Dave and Amy, brought the snowman to my attention. Since then, Allander has possessed the body of a young girl. And, he is very difficult to banish."

"And the police are on your case because of his killings?" Woodlin asks.

"Aye," Ránulf answers. "And he'll keep on killin'. I can't cast him out—magic's not strong enough for that. But maybe ye can summon the power of thy Wiccan gods?"

"In a Circle with our highest coven, it may be possible," Isis says.

"But even if we summon the power to banish him," Woodlin says, "we cannot hold him in the Circle with us without him attacking us."

"Allow me to be in the Circle with thee and I shall do my best to contain him," Ránulf offers.

Later, Dave, Rowan, and Theena are walking in the forest near the house. It's still snowing.

"I can't believe it snowed this much in one night," Dave says.

"At least," Theena says, "without the hat, Allander can't become a snowman again."

"But being inside Angelique can be just as dangerous," Rowan says. Bast bounds behind them in the snow and jumps into Theena's arms. But, then her ears perk up and she hisses into the air.

"What's wrong, Bast?" Theena asks.

Angelique emerges from behind a tree.

"Greetings, you bitchin' witches," Allander's voice bellows from the frozen, zombified child.

Bast leaps incredibly from Theena's arms and attaches to Angelique's face. As Bast makes contact, Rowan closes the distance and cuts into the side of the undead girl with his consecrated sword.

Allander shrieks and tosses Bast away. He jumps back, out of range of Rowan's weapon. With a scowl, he glances at the feline familiar.

"How many lives do you have, cat?" Allander says with an evil grin. He gestures complexly and a red beam of energy travels from Angelique's hands to strike the hissing creature. On impact, Bast falls dead into the snow.

"No!" Theena cries as she begins to chant the spell for trapping undead. In her mind she pictures Allander perfectly immobile and in pain.

"Your magic is impressive," Allander taunts, "but like Rowena's, it is no match for mine."

Quicker than the blink of an eye, Angelique is on top of Theena, tearing at her with claws that form on the tips of her fingers. Theena screams, trying to cast a protective spell, but pain halts her effort.

In a flash, Rowan is on top of Angelique, trying to pry her dead hands from Theena's purpling neck.

"Dave! Help!" he cries.

Dave reaches for the weapon Rowan had given him earlier. A crossbow. Granted, not a very accurate weapon, but it was something Dave already knew how to use. He used to steal his father's and go hunting with Cory before he died. Now, instead of deer or rabbit, Dave was going to unload on a creature only whispered about. Dave loaded a bolt fashioned of rowan wood with a tip of silver. He has nine, all blessed by the high priest and priestess of the village.

"Rowan, stand clear," Dave warns.

Rowan lets go of Angelique and stands back. Before Rowan can say "Watch out for Theena," a bolt is buried in the base of Angelique's neck.

Allander screams an unholy sound none of them will ever forget. He forgets about Theena and clutches at the back of his neck. A blue light trickles around the wound. In a mad fury, Allander tears out the bolt, temporarily weakened.

Dave already has another prepared.

"No," Allander whispers, seeing Dave's weapon. It quickly glazes over with ice. Dave fires it, breaking the frozen bowstring and sending the rowan wood bolt harmlessly into the twilight sky.

Rowan stands over Theena, trying to guard his unconscious lover and tend to her wounds at the same time.

"Rowan," Dave stammers as Angelique approaches him. "The disk!"

Rowan reaches into his coat pocket and produces the disk with the fire runes.

"Die, spirit!" Rowan hisses as he lets the energy of his gods course through him into the amulet. Suddenly, fire erupts in a burning aura around Angelique's body.

Allander cries out for the third time and collapses.

"Dave," Rowan says quickly, "help me get Theena to the village. It's closer than the house."

They both grab hold of Theena and begin to walk towards the village.

Isis can't help but worry. *An evil spirit that Ránulf and Rowan can't handle?* With Rowena gone, she finds herself brooding this one out alone. Isis was more trained in the Craft than Rowena, thus her command, but Rowena had an edge of true sorcery that only she and Ránulf could hope to possess. Alas, if Woodlin weren't as hard-headed as he was, he, too, would feel Isis' dread. *There are going to be more deaths,* she thinks as she senses Rowan, Dave, and their unconscious companion approach. According to her divinations, one of these three was going to die and Theena was losing blood fast.

Bast lies watching the crumpled heap of Allander's host. *Why doesn't the Bearded Wizard just dispose of this being?* she wonders. *Too many have passed over the bridge of life due to its evil.*

She stands up as Angelique begins to move. She lingers long enough to see the shock on Angelique's frozen face.

"Fucking cat!" moans Allander in resignation. "Why won't you die?"

Smiling to herself, yet feeling determined, Bast races off toward the house… and Ránulf.

Timbre came bounding towards Theena in the warm, spring meadow. The wolf's tongue was lolling to one side, lazily. The beast stopped when she reached Theena, her head quizzically cocked to one side.

How Theena loved her familiar… but she knew this wasn't real. Regardless of how real the hurt was, she still knew. Allander had beaten her and sent her to this limbo. She knew it was time for her to cross the bridge to the land of eternal summer.

Timbre's eyes sparkled inwardly.

No, Theena, came the reply from Timbre.

Theena's eyes began to fill with tears. She couldn't bear to see her familiar and friend here before her now.

Timbre spoke again in Theena's mind.

Do not mourn me, kind one. Yours is not the time to Cross the Bridge. You are loved and needed by others. Return now and—

"Wake up, Theena!" It was Rowan.

Theena opens her eyes.

"Timbre," she whispers.

"Oh, Theena!" Rowan kisses her.

The witches in the village used their herbs and healing magic to the best of their ability to cure Theena's wounds. It was their turn to heal the healer who had spent so much time by their bedsides. It is close to midnight and Rowan sits in a chair next to her bed. Isis, the village priestess, was there, too. Rowan smothers Theena with kisses.

"I didn't know if you would make it, my love." Tears fall freely down his face.

"Neither did I, at first," Isis admits, heavily.

"Dave went back to the house around 9:00 to tell Ránulf what happened," Rowan announces.

"Alone?" Theena tries to sit up.

Rowan gently eases her back down.

"No," he reassures her. "Woodlin has accompanied him."

"The evil in the air is very thick this night," Isis mutters. "Can you both feel it?"

Rowan and Theena both nod sadly at the 48 year-old high priestess, sensing her expertly hidden fear and noting her worry.

"It is hard to believe that evil would manifest itself in such a loving and gods-worshipping place," Isis says, "but I must get the Cirde prepared for our visiting demon."

Ránulf is back in his library turning page after page in his books.

"Something *must* be here!" he cries in frustration. He is clutching his black-handled athame. Matt enters the room.

"What's wrong?" he asks.

"I must be getting old," Ránulf laments. "A year ago I could have had Allander's ghost done away with instantly. But ever since Rowena died my magics have been getting weaker. I just don't know what to do."

"After Allander is dealt with," Matt says, "I think you should go on vacation. You haven't been back to Yorkshire to see Karine for twenty years. She doesn't have too much time left in our world."

"The old crone has more life in her than ye think, Matthew," Ránulf says, chuckling. "Yet, all she has left now is her vampire-hunting grandson killing off alleged lycanthropes and taking down cosmic death cults. It is an idea, however. I *should* go see Stonehenge one last time before they close it in preference of a replica, anyway."

Bast rubs against Ránulf's leg, purring.

"What is it, Ubasti?" he asks, picking her up.

Bast's eyes are filled with questions.

"I understand thy confusion, kitten," he says with a sigh, "but only the gods know the outcome of this situation."

Oddly enough, Woodlin and Dave reach the house safe and unaccosted at 9:30. Ránulf is stricken ill with the news of Theena. With prayers to the God and Goddess, they go to bed by 11 that night. All are haunted by uncomfortable dreams. Dave, in his inexperience, suffers the worst of the nightmares. In them, Jacob Allander cleverly is weakening Dave's spiritual resistance. Dave's mind would soon be open for the taking.

Chapter 48

Angelique is walking through a forest outside of Ránulf and the witches' property. Allander must take in the coldness and the ice as his energy. He had to leave the wizard's estate because everything there is blessed and protected by the fucking witches. But here, the cold is neutral and uncaring, perfect for Allander's sustenance. As the first rays of the morning sun try to pierce through the clouds, Allander realizes it will be a very cold and snowy day. He laughs inside Angelique's former body. It's a good day to kill some witches.

Ránulf and Woodlin are up at dawn.

"You don't believe that destroying Angelique's body will destroy Allander?" Woodlin asks.

"No," Ránulf confides. "Otherwise he would have been more affected when Kim, Rowan, Theena, and Dave burned the hat."

Dave walks into the room, pale from lack of sleep.

"We tried for so long to get that hat," Dave says, "but it didn't help worth shit."

"Ah," Ránulf says. "There ye are wrong! Do ye see any ax-wielding snowmen running around?"

"Dave," Woodlin interjects, sounding concerned. "You look sick. What's the matter?"

"No sleep." Dave sits in the living room with them. "Dreams about Amy, Angelique, and Allander."

"I think it's time ye had another dose of that purification potion," Ránulf says. "Ye are in ripe condition for possession. Stay inside today."

Dave stares into the warming fire. It seems to mock him. He shivers.

"Why is it so cold in here?" Dave asks.

"Woodlin and I have determined that when fire burned the hat, the fireplace and chimney suffered a curse." Ránulf frowns.

"We burned it downstairs," Dave says.

"It's all the same chimney," Woodlin says. "And now none of the fires are giving off heat."

"How's Theena?" Dave changes the subject.

"Matt left about fifteen minutes ago to go to the village and check," Woodlin says.

"Did anybody go with him?" Dave asks.

"No," Ránulf replies. "He took his truck. My divinations said Theena would be okay, though."

"There's a priestess in South Dakota that I know," Woodlin says. "She's not a traditional Wiccan because she ignores the God, but she's very close to the Goddess and has great powers of goodness. It is said that no evil spirits can be summoned in her presence or in her town."

"Oh, yes," Ránulf recalls with a smile. "Lady Wolven. She also has the service of plants and the animals of the forest. Aye, she is very formidable. Unfortunately, she is very unwilling to leave her home in the mountains. She's operating on one of my old estates."

"Let me speak with her," Woodlin says. "She has no phone, but one of Rowan's ravens can go to her."

As if summoned, the ravens gather at the living room window and respond with a few *clicks* and *caws*. The sounds then grow furious.

"Rowan's in trouble," Ránulf says and runs to the library. He grabs his athame and his staff.

Woodlin wraps his cloak around him.

"The village has been endangered," he says, ominously. "I can feel it."

Dave puts on his coat and takes his crossbow.

"Shit, I forgot to fix the bowstring when I thawed this out." He leaves the crossbow but brings the rowan-wood bolts. The three of them pile into Ránulf's Suburban. They drive without speaking, but

Woodlin is preparing a message on a small piece of paper from his Rite in the Rain notebook.

Lady Wolven,

We at the covenstead near Omaha require your blessings. The undead form of Jacob Allander has returned to haunt us. Too many have died by his undead hands. By now you have heard of Rowena's passing. Even Ránulf is helpless against Allander. We beg of you, Lady, aid us.

Blessed Be,
Woodlin

The message is rolled and placed in a small plastic film canister as they drive onto the road that leads to the village. The snow begins to fall heavily. Ránulf speaks.

"I don't think Matthew made it to the village," he says.

Dave begins to ask "'Why not" when he sees Matt's truck pulled over on the side of the road.

"I don't sense danger," Woodlin whispers. Ránulf stops the Suburban near the truck.

"No," he says. "Allander is gone, now."

The three get out and go to the truck. Matt is unconscious, leaning over the steering wheel. Blood runs down his face. His chest is torn up and pumping out blood freely.

"David," Ránulf says and clears his throat. "Get in and follow us to the village. The keys are still in the ignition."

Woodlin and Ránulf get back in the Suburban and head down the road to the witches' village.

Semi-digested material tries in vain to erupt through Dave's esophagus. Instead, Dave holds it in and gently moves Matt over to the passenger side. In horror, he sees blood has covered his hands.

Dave starts the engine and pulls back onto the road. That's when he sees the smoke coming from the village.

Oh no! he thinks. *The village is on fire!*

Ránulf and Woodlin reach the destruction first. The central building and the stables are on fire. The stench of charred animal flesh—*horrible, but please let it only be animal*s, Ránulf hopes - fills the air. Three other fires are being brought under control. Ránulf hurries to the stables and concentrates on his spellcasting. *Fire, you are starved. Air and wood and straw turn from you.* The flames soon begin to die as they fail to find purchase on any fuel needed to spread.

The fires in the central building die without Ránulf's assistance due to charms and wards already placed on the structure. Being the target of Christian violence, the witches in the village lived in a perpetual state of defense and hypervigilance.

Isis and Rowan meet Ránulf.

"He came running through the village an hour ago causing several buildings to set on fire," Rowan informs him.

"Casualties?" Ránulf asks, breathlessly.

"Livestock." Rowan sighs.

"How could he start anything on fire?" Ránulf asks. "He feeds on frost! Fire is contradicting to his power."

"He didn't create the flames!" Isis spits out through clenched teeth. "He caused all lanterns, hearths, and candles to spread their flames. This village would be nothing but cinders if the gods weren't watching over us."

"Thank thy gods then, Isis," Ránulf says. "How fares Theena?"

"She slept through all of it," Rowan says. "Isis gave her something to help her sleep and aid in her healing."

"Speaking of sleeping," Ránulf says to Rowan. "Did ye have any discomforting dreams last night?"

"No. Why?" Rowan asks.

"Allander is trying to break Dave mentally," Ránulf warns. "He is a prime suspect for possession."

As they speak, Dave drives Matt's truck into the village.

"Get yer healers to that truck, Isis," Ránulf says, urgently. "Matthew is dying."

Dave gets out of the truck and stares. Several witches attend to Matt.

"Come with me and we'll get you washed up," Rowan says as he approaches Dave.

Dave looks down at himself. He's drenched in Matt's blood. He sways in revulsion, daring to faint. Rowan puts an arm around Dave to steady him. They go to the cabin where Theena is recovering. The small, three-roomed structure is where Theena and Rowan stay when they are in the village.

"Theena is asleep and recovering in the room we usually use for *her* patients. I didn't want to disturb her when getting into my things," Rowan informs Dave. "I put a cool, antique bath in our room a few months ago and filled it with hot water before the attack. It was for Theena, but looking at you, my friend, I think you need it more."

They go into his and Theena's room. Dave chuckles at the contrast between the relaxed atmosphere of intimate relationships among the witches compared to Ránulf's more *parental* sensibilities.

"Does Ránulf know you both share a room here in the village?" Dave asks.

"Aye," says Ránulf as he comes in through the bedroom door, "and I also know what ye and thy lass did on the living room couch the other day." He throws Rowan a mischievous look that causes him to flush bright red.

"How do you keep walking in during the middle of people's sentences and finish them?" Dave mumbles, trying to find a moment of humor in an otherwise dark day.

Rowan clears his throat and turns back to Dave.

"Take off your bloody clothes and I'll be right back in," Rowan says as he and Ránulf return to the common room. Rowan walks to the door of the room Theena is in and looks back at Ránulf, whose eyes have never left him.

"What?" Rowan asks, finally. Ránulf joins him to look in on Theena who is still sleeping.

"Nothing, lad." Ránulf laughs to himself. "Ye'll make a good high priest to this village some day."

"We've discussed it a million times, Ránulf," Rowan says, exhausted, as if on autopilot. "I want to be a Wiccan priest. True, I find your magic fascinating, but I would rather be here, supporting the villagers, serving the Lord and Lady, instead of being buried in books at the house—" He pauses. "Wait. Did you say 'high priest'? Not 'high mage'?"

"I reckon I did," Ránulf says, "but ye can never be too sure I'm worth my salt." He gives Rowan a grin and departs to check back in with the villagers on the fire damage.

Rowan returns to his room where Dave waits. Dave stands in

his briefs awaiting Rowan.

"You'll have to take those off to get in here," Rowan says, looking at the bath.

Dave slips out of his underwear and gets into the water.

"It *is* still warm," Dave says, sinking to his neck in the deep tub. He can feel his skin begin to tingle. "What's in the soup?" he asks.

"On the bottom you'll find an herb sachet," Rowan says, pulling over a chair. "I hope you don't feel too self-conscious about me watching you bathe, but I have a few things to tell you."

"I don't care as long as I can watch you bathe sometime," Dave says with a laugh. He takes a cloth from Rowan and begins to scrub away Matt's blood.

"In that sachet," Rowan begins, "are various healing herbs. Eucalyptus, peppermint, rose, vervain, and lemon balm just to name a few. Of course they were meant for Theena, but I have more." Rowan produces a tiny vial of oil. "This is a protection oil," he announces as he pours some into the bath. "Rosemary, rose geranium, and cypress oils are some of the essences used to make it. Due to your dreams, I think it will help you."

"Thanks," Dave says before going under to rinse his hair. When he comes up, Rowan is leaving and Ránulf has returned.

"I brought ye this," Ránulf says, a little serious. "Rowan makes a good protective oil but this will relate to ye better."

Ránulf dumps another oil into the water.

"Start throwing the carrots and celery in at any time," Dave says.

"I am no cannibal," Ránulf replies with a mock *harrumph*. "The oil contains frankincense, myrrh, lavender, and clove." He turns to go but turns back to Dave with a wry look. "Clove *is* arousing so I will tell Rowan that it is not him which is causing thy stimulation. At least, I *think* it's not him. Soak thyself in there for a while. Tha'll not be gettin' possessed tonight—not unless Allander fancies bubble baths."

Ránulf leaves as Rowan comes back in.

Dave notices the herbs taking effect as blood begins to fill his penis.

Rowan stands over the bath with a towel and some homespun clothing. Dave rises and Rowan glances at his erection, momentarily surprised.

"Ránulf put lavender and clove in the water," Dave says, his turn to go beet red. "Uhhh, what's a boner between dudes, I guess?" He laughs.

"'Dudes,'" Rowan quotes. "You don't hear that word too much around here." He hands Dave the towel. "Here. Dry that monster off."

"No?" Dave says, drying off. "You just hear a lot of 'ye' and 'thy'? I kid, but I think Ránulf sounds cool talking like that." He puts on the homespun pants and shirt, then a wool cloak.

"I'd say you'd like rural England, then, but none of the other British people I've met speak that way, either. By the way, Ránulf says we'll be here in the village most of the day," Rowan informs him.

Isis knocks on Rowan's door and enters.

"Where did Ránulf say he was going?" she asks.

"Nowhere," Dave and Rowan both answer.

"Well, he just took off walking into the forest and a full-blown snow storm is brewing," she informs them.

In a nearby cabin, Woodlin ties the film canister containing his message to Lady Wolven onto a raven's leg.

"Fly to the Lady when the snow breaks, my friend," he says to the bird. "She is expecting you and the gods will watch over you."

Woodlin leaves his window ajar and wraps his cloak around him. He goes outside to where an arranged pile of wood is set on the ground. Calling upon the gods he strikes a long match and sets fire to the wood. He reaches into a pouch and withdraws a palmful of herbs and salt which he throws into the fire. His thoughts and magic are centered on one thing: halting the snowfall.

The snow stops before he even expects it. The raven exits the window of his cabin and takes to the chilled air.

In the forest, Ránulf approaches a clearing.

In the forest, also, Allander is wandering within Angelique's otherwise empty form. His thoughts, if you can call them thoughts in a shade without a biological, working mind, are consumed with revenge. Kim Batchons approaches Angelique from behind holding a black staff and a dagger.

"A *very* poor attempt at invisibility," Allander taunts.

"Return to your Hell," Batchons threatens.

"Never," Allander turns toward Batchons, grinning. "Come to your death so soon, my former student?"

"No, Jacob," Batchons says, "but to cease your undeath and to return you to your grave."

Allander weaves a spell and unleashes his purple flames towards Batchons. Kim waves his staff and the violet light is contained within it. With an incredible amount of will, Kim transfers the spell through his dagger and back at Allander. To Kim's surprise, Allander dispels the sorcery and cackles hideously.

In the tradition of the snowman, Angelique produces an ax from seemingly nowhere.

"This I will enjoy," Allander teases.

Suddenly, Kim's dagger flies through the air and pierces Angelique's chest.

Allander begins to scream, but finishes with maniacal laughter.

"Maybe if this dagger was consecrated with light instead of evil, Batchons," Allander howls with a laugh. He pulls the dagger out of his host's chest.

"Nyarlathotep!" cries Kim Batchons as violet flames of his own erupt from his staff.

"Not again," hisses Allander. He gestures at Kim Batchons and casts a spell, muting him with spectral sorcery.

Kim chokes. *My voice!* Fighting panic, he lets his flames sear into Angelique's undead body.

How stupid, Allander thinks, as his host body flies into the snow.

"Your magic cannot harm me, Batchons!" Allander bellows, immediately standing back upright. Suddenly, Ránulf is behind Angelique throwing clear liquid from a vial all over the back of the frozen, undead child.

Allander bellows in rage, as charred pieces of dead flesh fall from Angelique's smoking back. Allander looks from Ránulf to Batchons, pauses a beat, and then flees.

Batchons casts a spell to hold undead in their place, but Allander ignores it as he flees into the trees. The snow begins to fall again.

"What did you do to him, wizard?" Batchons asks.

Ránulf holds up his vial.

"Holy water, Kimberly," Ránulf says with a cat-ate-the-canary smile. "My own version."

"Don't refer to me as 'Kimberly', old man," Batchons nearly spits. "Did you see? My magic isn't working on him any more!"

"Of course not," Ránulf says, "Ye both thrive on darkness and evil. The only thing that will counter Allander will come from the Light!"

"Light?" mocks Batchons. "Shit went down in the Light, Wylkyn. Or haven't you been there lately? Destroy Angelique's body and Jacob will have nowhere to go."

"I know what I am going to do to rid the world of Allander," Ránulf says. "Thy aid is no longer required. Kindly depart." He turns from Kim Batchons and starts to walk away.

"Don't turn away from me, mage," Batchons snarls, preparing a spell of stunning.

"That would be extremely unwise, Kimberly," Ránulf warns.

"Don't call me that!" Batchons screams as he unleashes his magic at the old wizard.

Ránulf waves the magic away and splashes some of his consecrated water into Batchons' face where it quickly freezes.

"You fucker!" Kim cries. He starts towards Ránulf with his staff raised, but Ránulf mutters something under his breath and Batchons promptly falls into the snow in a sudden, deep slumber.

When he awakens, Kim is in his home on his living room floor. His meeting with Ránulf is vague in his mind.

That was incredibly dumb thought Kim to himself. *Why did I threaten Wylkyn? I could use him as a potential ally against Allander and learn the secrets of his magic in the process.* Kim was forced to admit it, Ránulf may lack in magical offense, but his other talents were extraordinary. For instance, how did Kim get back to his home when he was only at Ránulf's fifteen minutes ago? It's a half hour drive from his house.

While Kim Batchons was home, lost in thought, Allander neared the village. From his vantage point, Allander could see Dave walking with a witch on the outskirts of the village. Allander reached into Dave's mind.... and recoiled with a shock.

He's protected! thought Allander in anger. *Well, we'll just see for how long.*

Dave feels a sharp pain inside his head.

"What's wrong?" asks Teresa, the witch accompanying him.

"I don't know," Dave ponders. "The back of my head hurts."

"We can go to your cabin and get something for it," Teresa suggests.

"No," Dave says. "I'll be fine. How's Matt holding up?"

"He's pretty critical," Teresa says, sadly. "I think he'll have to be taken into Omaha for medical treatment."

Lightning dances across the cold winter sky. Thunder quickly follows.

"That's not a good sign is it?" Dave asks, looking up into the sky.

"It's good and bad," Teresa says. "It's a sign from the gods. We can tap the storm for its magical energy, but it's also bad that we're gonna need it."

Lightning flares again. Dave and Teresa walk back into the heart of the village. Ránulf returns to the village at the same time. He meets Rowan, Isis, and Woodlin in Woodlin's cabin.

"It must be done tonight," Isis says.

"Some of the coven are starting a bonfire in the center of the village," Woodlin says. "We've got all the herbs, oils, and stones we will need."

"We must get rid of this walking corpse tonight," Isis nearly moans. "If we don't, there will be no stopping this monstrosity."

"Aye," Ránulf says. "We'll do it tonight. Allander is just outside the village as we speak."

Naturally, Ránulf is correct. As he speaks, Allander-as-Angelique is building a crude snowman.

Won't this be a scare? Allander thinks. He pushes the snowman toward the village and it slides effortlessly, picking up speed. The snowman enters the village on a heading towards Rowan and Theena's cabin. It jets by several villagers and passes them before they even register what they are seeing.

Inside the cabin, Theena has awakened and is talking to Dave.

"Where's Rowan?" Theena asks.

"I don't know, actually," Dave replies. "I imagine he's in the village, but I don't know where."

"Is anyone at the house?" Theena asks.

"Not that I know of," Dave says.

Thunder cracks overhead once more as the snowman suddenly stops in front of the cabin. From inside, Theena and Dave hear a tapping at the door.

"I'll get it," Dave says as he leaves Theena's recovery room.

In Woodlin's cabin, there are seven witches. Among them are Rowan, Woodlin himself, and Isis. These are the most experienced Wiccans in the village.

Woodlin brings the coven to attention.

"Tonight, we must banish a lethal spirit from our world," Isis says to the group. The five coveners sit at a table, Woodlin and Isis are standing before them.

"This evil entity is unlike anything we've ever encountered," Isis continues. "The spirit has possessed the body of a young girl, I'm told. Her soul has passed on, but we can't get rid of the entity by destroying its host. It must be exorcised first."

"Ránulf has asked us to banish it," Woodlin adds. "He will contain the body and spirit within our Circle while we work our magic. After the banishing, the body will be consecrated into our bonfire."

"I know we're not at *full* power," Isis says, "but Amergin won't be back from his trip to South Dakota for the New Year's Eve Blue Moon for two days."

"We can't wait that long," Rowan speaks up. "It almost killed Theena yesterday."

"Shea," Isis says to one of the women present, "I would like you to mind the censer. I've mixed a very powerful exorcism incense with eleven different herbs in it."

Isis hands Shea the packet of powdered incense. The 34 year-old witch puts the packet in her pocket. The incense contains *Angelica archangelica*, asafoetida, way bennet, sweet basil, frankincense, fumitory, heliotrope, juniper, myrrh, rosemary, and rue.

Woodlin hands a 39 year-old male witch with brown hair a stick from a birch tree.

"Dylan," Woodlin says to him. "At my word you must strike the violated body with this branch."

Dylan nods his head in understanding.

"Deanna," Isis says, looking at a 40 year-old woman with brown hair, "on the shelf behind you, you will see a sack filled with elder leaves and berries. At the proper time, I need you to toss handfuls of them onto the girl's body."

Woodlin hands a small jar of ointment to a 29 year-old woman with black hair.

"This is mallow ointment," Woodlin says. "As the body becomes immobile this needs to be rubbed into the skin, especially the face and head. Will you do that, Stefnia?"

"Got it," she says.

"What do I get to do?" Rowan asks.

"Well," Isis says, "Ránulf recommends that you stuff the girl's mouth with salt and a bulb of garlic."

"How will the possessed be immobilized so we can do all of this?" Shea asks.

"That's up to Ránulf," Isis replies.

Back at the main house, it is not quite as deserted as Dave had suggested. Well, it's hardly his fault. One can hardly be blamed for being incorrect when things happen outside our immediate awareness.

Angelique bursts through a window in Ránulf's library, sending pieces of what was once an attractive work of stained glass scattering across the floor. Of course, even at the village, Ránulf is immediately aware of her presence in his private space, but he is rather busy at the moment. Allander feels the magic protection and quickly summons his reserves of energy to continue to enter the house. Out of everything in Ránulf's library, he heads for the phone.

In the village, Dave approaches the door to the cabin and opens it. He screams in terror at the sight of the snowman. The being of snow flies at Dave, knocking him to the floor. The snowman crumbles as Dave passes out.

"Dave?" Theena cries in a fearful voice. She tries to sit up, but pain tears through her chest and she lies back down. "Dave?! What's wrong?"

Ránulf enters the cabin and closes the open door.

"It's all right, Theena," he says. "I'll take care of it."

Ránulf kneels beside Dave.

"David," he says. "Pick thyself up."

"What's going on?" Theena asks from the room.

"David has had a fright and appears to have fainted."

Dave begins to awaken. Upon seeing Ránulf he exclaims, "A snowman! It jumped at me!"

"I know," Ránulf says. "It was a diversion. Allander is at the house."

"At the house?" Dave asks. "Doing what?"

"I don't rightly know," Ránulf says, "but it's time to end his existence. I'm telling ye now to stay away from the Circle, but I know ye will want to observe. It will also be good learning for you, so ye may watch as long as ye are well secluded."

"You mean the High Coven is really going to get rid of Allander?" Dave asks.

"Aye," Ránulf says. "Tonight is the time—a night of great power. At midnight, we enter the second full moon of December. December 31. A Blue Moon."

He turns with a wry glance. "Ye'll excuse me while I cast a necro-being from my home?"

With that, he disappears into Rowan's room and shuts the door.

Angelique's corpse reaches for the phone. Allander hasn't used a telephone in 13 years. Where was the dial? Why didn't the phone have a sticker with the 7-digit number for the county sheriff's office on it? Even if he remembered Omaha's number, it would be long-distance from here, wouldn't it? Omaha wasn't set up yet on the new 119 system in 1977 but it had to be by now, right? Or was it 991?

Well, we'll just try the operator, won't we? Allander thinks as he presses the "0" on the touch-tone phone.

A female voice answers with, "Operator" and "How may I help you?"

"May I have the number for police emergencies?" Allander asks.

"You mean 911?" the operator asks.

"Yes." Allander smiles. "That will do fine." He presses down the hook switch to disconnect. He releases it and places the receiver at his ear as he presses 9-1-1.

"Emergency," a male voice says bluntly after two rings.

Summoning the use of Angelique's vocal chords, Allander screams into the phone.

"Help me! You've gotta help me! I need the police!"

"What's the matter, honey?" the 911 operator asks. "Calm down and tell me where you are."

"On an estate," Angelique's voice says, crying frozen alligator tears. "The one with the witches' village."

"What's the problem?" the man asks.

"I've been kidnapped by them! They're taking me to the village tonight. They're gonna kill me!"

"What's your name, dear?" the man asks. "I need to know your name."

"Oh," says Angelique/Allander in a hushed tone. "I gotta go. The old man with the beard is coming!"

Allander laughs to himself as he hangs up the phone. *Well done,* he thinks. He can feel Ránulf's magic working against him so he quickly exits the way he came. *Time to destroy that old son-of-a-bitching wizard.*

Chapter 49

Steve Pellon is on desk duty. Ever since that wolf killed Tony out at the Devil's Ranch, the Sheriff hasn't allowed Steve back in a cruiser. Paperwork and more paperwork with an extra side of paperwork greeted Steve every evening. Tonight, he manned the phones.

Why was he the only one to see what was going on? Five cops, dead. One mauled by a wolf, two run off the road by a semi, and two drove into the Missouri River? *Of course Wylkyn was responsible.* Him and his Satanic sidekick, Rowan. A bullet was found in Officer Tate's chest *and* they were found in the backseat of their cruiser. *Murder suicide by her jealous lover, my ass!*

Then what about the crazy bitch who was found on her snowy lawn as her house burned down? he thought. Cheryl Merring was her name. She was found babbling about how some man made out of ice tried to choke and beat her to death. The body of her daughter, Amy, still hasn't been found. Her son, Ricky, had been grotesquely mutilated and dropped on her doorstep two days before. He was in a huge, gift-wrapped box. Ránulf Wylkyn and Kim Batchons both were involved in that one, for sure. Cheryl's down in the state sanitorium in Lincoln now, singing "Frosty the

Snowman" on repeat in the most horrific voice Steve had ever heard emanate from a human being.

The phone rang, bringing Steve back to reality.

"Emergency," he says bluntly into the receiver.

The call had really shaken him up.

So, Wylkyn is going to have his witches sacrifice an innocent girl tonight? Steve hangs up and steps away from his workstation.

"Steve?" the other operator on duty asks. "Where are you going?"

"Shut up, Margo," Steve snaps at her, then smiles. "I'm going to go finally bust some devil worshippers."

With that, Steve storms out of the office. Luckily, he still has the keys to his cruiser. He checks his gun, then starts the car. He flips on his lights and siren and heads toward the estate.

Margo calls the sheriff and he finds someone to take Steve's post. He checks the system to see where Steve's last emergency call came in from.

A good twelve minutes pass between the time Steve left the station and the time Sheriff Michael Farrens calls out an All Points Bulletin on him. At this point, Steve is eighteen minutes out from the estate. Two minutes past his arrival would put him at the village just in time for Isis' fatal premonition. Theena? Dave? Rowan? Too much can happen in just twenty minutes.

Chapter 50

Allander is running Angelique towards the village.

This will be great, Allander thinks. *When the cops get here, they'll think the witches kidnapped me*. He laughs first to himself, then out loud into the night. "There's going to be trouble tonight!"

The seven Witches gather at the circle in the center of the village. Woodlin, Isis, Rowan, Deanna, Stefnia, Dylan, and Shea. Each has the ritual elements they require. The snow is falling slowly.

Ránulf silently joins the witches. They are wearing heavy cloaks of Earthen brown. All except Woodlin and Isis. Woodlin wears a cloak of black. Isis wears a cloak of white. Ránulf carries his rowan wood staff. He is wearing heavy robes of black with trims of white.

"Is everything prepared, priest and priestess?" Ránulf asks.

"Yes," Woodlin says. "All is in order."

"Summon the child, now, Ránulf," Isis says without emotion, her breaths becoming frost in the cold evening air.

Elsewhere, a phone rings.

Kim Batchons picks up his receiver and listens.

"Steve Pellon is on his way to Ránulf's estate right now," a woman's voice informs him. "A girl called 911 and said she was going to be sacrificed tonight."

"A prank," Kim replies. "Nothing more."

"Of course, sir," the woman on the other end says, "but the sheriff put out an APB to stop Pellon and then to check out the village and main house. Omaha is sending officers and Douglas county is preparing backup."

"You've done well, Margo," Batchons says. "Since OPD is going in first, it will be a while before they get there."

"Pellon will be there before them," Margo says. "Oh shit! A helicopter just went up. It's headed towards the estate."

"Thank you, Margo," Batchons says, quietly. "I'll handle it

from here." He hangs up.

That helicopter must be stopped. Damn! How convenient for me, though. Craig Carney just happens to be piloting tonight. Kim goes to a back room in his house. In the room is a desk with a CB radio on it. Kim turns it on and finds the channel needed to reach Carney in the helicopter.

Kim broadcasts three words, in a rough voice.

"Ingot. Fan-gae. Pingon."

Four people are in the helicopter.

"What the fuck was that?" one of them asks.

"I don't know," Carney's bewildered co-pilot replies.

"Repeat," Carney says into the receiver.

Nothing.

"Repeat," he says again.

Nothing.

"Air-1, what was that?" HQ radios in to ask.

"Unknown, base," Carney says.

Craig Carney knows those three words came from Kim Batchons. The words are no known language. Just spontaneously created by Batchons. Nevertheless, the meaning to Carney is dreadful and obvious. He must not let the helicopter reach Ránulf's estate.

"Kamikaze..." Carney whispers.

"What?" his co-pilot asks.

"Oh, nothing," Carney says and flashes his charming smile. *Goodbye Rebecca,* he thinks. Before he allows himself to reconsider, he cuts the helicopter's engine.

"Craig!" his co-pilot screams, taking the cyclic control to mitigate the spin as they go into autorotation. Carney empties several rounds from his firearm into his co-pilot.

The helicopter falls at high speed to the Earth and explodes in a ball of flame.

Chapter 51

Back at the village, Dave is sitting with Theena. They just finished eating soup from a thermos that Teresa brought over.

"Is Rowan participating in the thing tonight?" Theena asks.

"Don't know," Dave replies. "I hope this is the end of it, though."

"Oh, please let it be ended!" Theena exclaims, tears in her eyes. "I haven't even begun to process what and who we've lost. Geoff, Rowena, Timbre, Amy… all of the victims in the city. I am so angry that the laws of the universe and nature even permitted this all to happen."

Dave sighs, holding back tears himself. Sorrow fills him at the mention of those names and at seeing Theena so distressed.

"Well," Dave begins to suggest, quietly, "let's try to have a positive outlook. If our wills influence anything at all, this is the time we're going to need them."

"You're going to watch, aren't you?" Theena asks, looking him in the eye.

"I *do* like to watch," he says with a shrug and managing a grin. "You gonna be ok by yourself?"

"Mentally? No. Physically? Yes, I am feeling a little better and more rested."

For no apparent reason, Theena leans over and gives Dave a quick hug, surprising him.

"Be careful," she says, seriously. "I can't help but feel the danger, for you… and the others."

"I'll be careful," Dave says. Smiling, he adds, "And I'll keep an eye on Rowan, too."

He leaves Theena's room and pulls on his coat. He curses at himself under his breath as he remembers that he left his arrows in Ránulf's vehicle.

"Keep your protective aura up," Theena advises. She moves to the doorway to her room and stabilizes herself on the frame.

"I will," Dave says as he opens the door into the village night. "I'll ask Teresa to come over to keep you company for news and in case you need anything." Theena begins to protest, but Dave is out the door.

In the Circle, Ránulf and the High Coven begin.

"Jacob Allander!" cries Ránulf. "Infector of Angelique Barker, come to me! Ye are summoned before the Old Gods. Arrive, tainted one. Heed the call that ye cannot ignore!"

The energy pours out of Ránulf, crosses the distance instantaneously, and grapples Jacob Allander. Allander produces a cry of laughter and of pain.

"I come, Ránulf," he hisses. "I come."

Steve Pellon races unhindered towards the estate. His police radio is turned off.

Rowan's ravens settle uneasily in the trees near the village.

Another bird lies frozen in the snow of rural South Dakota. An unread message to Lady Wolven is attached to its foot.

Angelique/Allander nears the village, summoned by Ránulf's magic. *This will be our final meeting, mage*, he thinks, determination focusing his thoughts.

The snow continues to fall and the cold has formed icicles in Angelique's hair. Her skin is blue on account of being post-life combined with the falling temperature. She grasps firmly the blood-stained hatchet, having pulled it out of nowhere as was custom by now. The frozen skin on her face audibly crackles as she cracks a smile.

"Angelique took an ax and gave Ránulf Wylkyn forty whacks. She took a look at what she'd done and gave the fucker forty-one!"

Angelique cackles hideously and runs toward the village.

At the village, Shea walks deosil, or clockwise, around the circle with her burning incense.

"Woodlin," Ránulf says, "be ready. The dark child approaches the village."

Dave quietly slips between two buildings. He can see the witches beginning their ritual in the circle. He notices Ránulf, Rowan, Woodlin, and Isis, but the others are unknown to him. He rushes to a nearby bench and brushes it clear of snow where he sits to watch the proceedings. Bast appears and joins him.

Steve Pellon drives his cruiser onto the road leading to the village. His eyes are dazed as he speeds up the slick road.

The phone rings at Ránulf's manor. It finally stops after the 27th ring.

"Why doesn't that bastard get an answering service?" Kim Batchons yells out loud in his car. He shuts off his cellular phone. His car is about five minutes behind Pellon's.

Allander approaches the edge of the village in Angelique's body. He does not slow, instead he leaps into the air, bounding over the village buildings. He lands in the center of the witches' Circle, catching everyone off guard, except Isis.

"Hello!" greets Allander. "Oh what fun it is to go on a slaying spree tonight! Ha ha! Ha—".

Isis tosses a ritually-charged mixture of mullein and yarrow herbs into Angelique's exposed face.

Allander chokes and steps back, momentarily blinded.

Ránulf steps in front of Allander/Angelique holding his staff in one hand and a small, stone disk in the other.

"It is time for ye to leave this world once again, ye vile infection!" Ránulf says in a rage, spittle flying from his mouth.

Allander opens Angelique's eyes.

"You haven't the knowledge or *power* to get rid of me, Ránulf!" Allander shouts at the old man and laughs.

"Nay, ye are mistaken," Ránulf counters, more softly now due to the tightness in his chest as his emotions rise. He holds the stone disk, facing it towards Angelique. The disk has the rune for Earth inscribed on it. Ránulf's grip tightens around the disk. His chest burns, his breath ragged. He remembers Amy's scream—too late. He hears Geoff's final gasp. Too late. He sees Rowena's glowing, boiling eyes. Too late. But not again. Never again.

A tremendous amount of energy that Ránulf had been storing is finally released through the disk and amplified. His aura flares white, expanding outward—and for a moment, it takes the shape of a great raven with him at its center. Wings spread. Head feathers tuft. A radiant beam shoots from the outstretched disk, bathing Angelique and the space around her in a searing column of light.

The Earth around Angelique's feet ripples, sucking the animated corpse into the ground up to her knees.

"What?" Allander demands. "No!"

Isis and Woodlin begin to cast the Circle as the earth around

Angelique rises to trap her body where it stands. Her arms and legs are immobile.

From afar, Dave watches on in awe as Ránulf's namesake vanishes as quickly as it appeared. Ránulf returns the disk in a pocket of his robe.

Isis and Woodlin chant in unison, closing the High Coven inside liminal space within the finished, protective Circle.

"Deanna," Ránulf instructs, "the elder leaves!"

Deanna tosses elder leaves and berries onto Angelique. They scatter across her body and on the ground around it. Allander yells out in anger.

Carefully and quickly, Rowan shoves a humongous bulb of garlic into Angelique's mouth. Her eyes roll to the back of her head and she moans.

"The ointment, Stefnia," Isis says.

With motivated speed, Stefnia rubs mallow ointment onto Angelique's skin, starting with her face. Angelique's groan becomes a growl.

Deputy Pellon, *former-deputy* Pellon, he thinks at this point considering what he is about to do… shuts the engine off and gets out of his car. He removes his gun from its holster and unlatches the safety. He walks quickly towards the center of the village.

Did I just hear a car? Dave wonders. His attention is drawn back to the Circle as Rowan pours consecrated salt into Angelique's mouth and eyes from a glass vial. Allander's agony is acutely clear. The earth holding the possessed undead begins to crack under the strain.

Then, Dave sees something or someone in the shadows, moving towards the Circle from his left.

"A cop," Dave whispers, "with a gun..."

Bast rushes to the edge of the Circle and flashes a warning to Dylan.

Dave gets up, unnoticed, and works his way toward Pellon.

Pellon is staring intently at Ránulf. He doesn't see Dave approaching him from the side.

"Dylan," Ránulf says cautiously.

Dylan, disheveled by Bast's warning, sees Dave approaching Pellon.

"Ránulf," Dylan says, hushed.

"Never ye mind, Dylan," Ránulf insists.

"Dylan, the stick!" Woodlin commands. Dylan raises his birch stick and approaches Angelique. All the coveners channel their energy to the birchwood.

"You cannot kill winter, old man!" Allander yells, hysterically.

Pellon raises his gun and aims it at Dylan.

"No!" screams Dave.

Pellon turns and fires at Dave, startled by his outburst.

Dylan strikes the body of Angelique Barker with the birch cudgel.

From behind Pellon, Kim Batchons fires his own gun, cursing his timing.

Dave clutches his bloodied chest, cries out mutely, and falls to the ground, seemingly unconscious. Pellon falls on his face, dead.

Allander emanates a shrill, baneful shriek that does not belong to a child's throat. Angelique's limbs crack like ice and her claws gouge at the earth trapping her in place.

In an explosion of force, Allander attempts to flee Angelique's body. She implodes as he steps, whole, but not whole, from her body, holding the hatchet.

Dylan flies back and stumbles to the ground. Several of the coven cry out at the sight of Allander in their midst, free of Angelique's entrapments.

Without warning, Dave steps into the Circle without breaking it. He walks up behind Allander without disturbing any of the ground or snow and throws his arms around him. Allander drops his hatchet and turns within Dave's grasp to face him. Dave holds onto the spirit as the earth opens below them. Realizing what is about to occur, Allander screams in rage. The earth does not just swallow—it devours them. Dave grips Allander with all his might, dragging him down into the soil.

Suddenly, everything is quiet. The snow stops to let the moonlight illuminate the ghastly scene. The witches of the village begin to come out of their cabins, silent, reverent.

Ránulf, Rowan, and the coven all stare at the disturbed and blackened ground where Dave and Allander went under. Ránulf has tears in his eyes. The reflection of the moonlight is somehow strongest there and the light is playing tricks on him.

"Do you see him?" Rowan whispers to him.

As if made of the moonlight itself, Dave stands, weightless, above the broken ground. Moonlight fills the cracks in the earth and the ground is made whole again, the rift healed. He looks up and meets Ránulf's eyes. He smiles and then, is simply gone.

"Clear the Circle," Ránulf barely manages to choke out through his tears. Isis and Woodlin begin to uncast the Circle's protective border, ritually bestowing their gratitude to the elements of nature with a little extra emphasis on Earth this time.

Outside the Circle, Kim Batchons still kneels next to Dave.

Rowan grips Ránulf's arm to steady himself.

"How?" he asks.

"I've nowt but guesses, and they're not worth the candle," Ránulf says.

Ránulf and Rowan rush to join Kim at Dave's side. A sucking sound can be heard as Dave struggles to breathe.

"I'm no doctor, but I think it's pierced his lung," Batchons says.

Theena rushes through the village center and reaches Rowan. She stops as she sees Dave. She begins to weep, holding her stomach in distress. Dave gasps—a wet, rattling sound. Blood bubbles from his lips. He reaches for Rowan's hand, but his fingers tremble and fail. Rowan's hand finds purchase in his as he kneels beside him, his face pale.

"Stay with us, Dave. Just hold on." Theena presses a hand to his chest, trying to stem the bleeding, but the crimson stain spreads through her fingers.

Instructed by Isis, five witches cover Angelique's collapsed body with a woven blanket and carry her into the woods. A pyre has been prepared to burn the body.

Sirens can be heard as police vehicles approach. A helicopter searchlight begins to play across the village. The helicopter lands in a clear field next to the edge of the village. Three officers from the helicopter quickly take in the scene. One runs back to the 'copter to radio for a medevac.

As state and county police vehicles arrive, Ránulf returns to the circle to hide Angelique's hatchet in his robe before it is seen. The black buck stands on the horizon and in his mind, Ránulf hears him. *The willing heart given in love this night will protect the hearths of this coven for years to come.*

Epilogue

Several nights later, as the second full moon of December is waning into January, Rowan sits beside the spot where Dave's astral form had vanished. He doesn't speak. He doesn't cry. He just watches the snow fall, softer now, as if even the sky understood what had been given up to save them all.

Dave Langen did not survive. The medics did what they could, but the bullet had done its work. By the time the helicopter touched down at the hospital, he was already gone.

They held a quiet ceremony for him—just a few of them with his family, gathered in the cold air of the village. No grand speeches, no incantations. Just the wind through the trees and the heavy weight of grief.

Angelique Barker's body was burned, the ashes mixed with ceremonial salt and buried beneath consecrated earth. The ritual was done at dawn, with Isis leading the final rite. There was no mourning for her—only an uneasy silence, as if none of them were quite sure if they'd truly seen the last of Jacob Allander.

And yet, the cold weather finally lifted. The ice melted, and eastern Nebraska slipped into an unusually warm early January. Classic Nebraska 32 degree nights and 60 degree days. *If you don't like the weather, just wait 5 minutes*, he thinks.

Ránulf is already gone, off to England to reconnect with the Crone, Karine. After growing close with Dave, another "more distant stop" was in order. There were "overdue family matters better settled in his dotage than never." Mysterious, as ever.

The Covenstead Book and Metaphysical Supply Store has been put up for sale. Two buyers are interested. Neither of them are witches.

Rowan watches as members of the coven tend the animals and sacred grounds.

Mom, wherever you are now, please keep an eye on Dave and Amy. I bless you. I release you.

He rises and joins Dylan and Shea with their duties.

Postscript

Kim Batchons walked free. The jury saw only the death of a rogue deputy—not the deeper battle that had been fought in the shadows.

In the village, Amergin returned from South Dakota with the news that Woodlin's message never reached Lady Wolven. That knowledge lingers in the back of Woodlin's mind, unfinished.

In the weeks that followed, Theena committed to her training with Isis, determined to walk the path of the high priestess and healer. Rowan began formal studies in the Old Ways under Woodlin, now that Ránulf had released him from unspoken obligations to follow in the wizard's footsteps.

Matt took up the estate's day-to-day needs, becoming its unlikely steward and symbol of hope for a small community still recovering. With all who had been lost, his rebound after his injuries was nothing short of miraculous.

The police have closed the case on the Christmas hatchet-murders. There will be no more questions, no more investigations. The horror of that winter is already fading into rumor, a story to be twisted and sensationalized on late-night TV specials.

But for now, the town breathes, unaware that the world still turns toward its next nightmare.

THE END

December 15, 1991—WW

www.ingramcontent.com/pod-product-compliance
Lightning Source LLC
Chambersburg PA
CBHW020742020826
48980CB00019B/701/J

* 9 7 9 8 9 9 8 6 8 1 0 3 5 *